THE GOLD OF ISHMAEL: THE ADVENTURES OF JOHN SOLOMON, VOLUME 12

H. BEDFORD-JONES

THE GOLD OF ISHMAEL

THE ADVENTURES OF
JOHN SOLOMON, VOLUME 12

H. BEDFORD-JONES

COVER BY
PAUL STAHR

ILLUSTRATIONS BY
ROGER B. MORRISON

STEEGER BOOKS • 2025

THE GOLD OF ISHMAEL

CHAPTER I

ENTER JOHN SOLOMON

IT CERTAINLY is funny how you run into people. Here I was in Morocco—I had come down from Algiers across the whole country—and flattered myself that I did not know a soul in all Casablanca. I walked around the corner from the hotel, and went to a café to get a drink, and there was Tom Keyes sitting at a table as large as life.

"My gosh! It's Hank Smith or I'm a Dutchman!" he cried, and we shook hands. "What on earth are you doing here? I thought you were back in Chicago or somewhere writing newspaper stories and uplifting the human race. Heard you got married last year. Where's the wife?"

"Divorced," I said, just to let him have the news straight. "She turned out to be a paranoiac, tried to have me locked up for lunacy, raised hell generally. I divorced her, got a commission to do some stories on Algiers and Morocco, and here I am, a sadder and wiser man, free as a bird and ready to paint the town red. Let's have a drink."

"Let's have six," said Keyes. "Got ten thousand francs on you? Or can you raise it?"

"Can't raise passage home until I cable," I said. "I've got the equivalent of forty dollars in African money. Ten thousand francs! Gosh, no! Why aren't you selling automobiles in Denver?"

"Because I'm selling 'em here. Invested my life's savings in the North Africa agency, see? And, Hank—listen! Don't ever take on anything in foreign parts. I've been here a year; and what they do to you when you're not looking is a crime—"

Come to find out, Tom Keyes was down on his luck, but he was not whining about it. He did not look mined and he did not act ruined, and as a matter of fact he was not ruined—he was just three hours ahead of it. At five that same afternoon he would be sitting in jail, unless his unpaid bills were met. There was not the least chance of their being met, and jail in Morocco is not operated as a philanthropy. It is meant to be unpleasant, and it succeeds.

Keyes looked cheerful enough—he always did. He had a wide-eyed way of looking at the world which inspired confidence; dark hair, gray eyes, a hearty laugh, medium build. All in all, a sensible, solid sort. Not at all like me. I stand six foot one stripped, am long and lean and skinny, with a broken nose that was never set right and a habit of frankness which may be refreshing but does not make the wrong sort of people like me. A heart of gold, you understand, but nevertheless a general air of cussedness, as I have been informed at various times; if you want to believe my late unlamented better half, Hank Smith is an undiluted brute. Suit yourself.

We tried to figure things out, while before us surged all the astonishing life of the Place de France. Here in Casablanca, the chief port of Morocco, met the old life and the new, at right angles—shuffling Arabs, trim French officers, Jews with flowing robes and black caps, horses, autos, trucks going to and from the rocks, large and small autobusses. Across from us rose the old walls of the native quarter or medina, in sharp contrast to the newly opened branch of a great Paris department store. And Arabs everywhere, hitching their awkward jellabs up over one shoulder, white Arabs, black Arabs and all the colors in between flowing past us.

Raising the money was out of the question for me, my account being already overdrawn. Hank Smith seldom has any money; my philosophy is that wealth is good for only one thing—to make you comfortable. I was comfortable enough, and broke. I

plied Keyes with all sorts of suggestions, but he had overlooked no bets. He was through, done for.

So there we sat. At a pinch, I might help; I could go to the consulate, show my papers, and have him cable for the money on the plea that I was the one in debt. It would mean losing my job, but that was better than letting Tom Keyes go to jail.

Of course, the two of us were conspicuous enough, since American business men always stand out with sharp distinction from tourists or Frenchmen. Thus, if anybody were looking for Tom Keyes, even a stranger, and knew about where to find him, there was nothing at all odd in his coming straight to us. And come he did.

A QUEER little man came up to the table, with an apologetic air, and took the third chair.

"I don't suppose, sir, as 'ow you 'ave a match?" he said to Keyes. "This danged pipe won't keep a-going, and a good match is werry 'ard to find in foreign parts, as the old gent said when 'e buried 'is third. Thank 'ee, sir—"

Keyes handed over a box of matches. I took a second look at the speaker.

He was a pudgy little old man with gray hair, a blank and expressionless face—not unlike the faces of Arabs, in that it had no lines or wrinkles—and very wide and blank eyes of sky blue. He was carelessly dressed, smoked a vile old clay pipe, and wore a black Basque beret, though he was obviously no Frenchman. I put him down as engineer or assistant chief on some ship in harbor.

"I was told, sir," he said, when he had his pipe alight, "as 'ow I'd find a gent name o' Keyes a-sitting 'ere. I don't suppose by any chance one of you is 'im?"

When those mild blue eyes met mine, I received a slight sense of shock. They seemed to go clear into my brain, as it were. Their blank appearance was deceptive.

"Why, yes, I'm Keyes," said Tom. "The office told you I'd be here, eh?"

The pudgy little man nodded, and I noticed that he seemed to be looking me over with a good deal of interest.

"Yes sir, just like that. I've saved up a bit o' tin, Mr. Keyes, and I am thinking of putting my money into the automobile business. I ain't as young as I was once, and I 'ave a business of me own in Paris, but me 'eart went back on me, so to speak. Go to Morocco, the doctor says, and set in the sun and do nothing, all winter. But a man 'as got to be doing of something, as the old gent said when 'e kissed the 'ousemaid."

Keyes was obviously astonished by this information. I kicked his ankle under the table, but he only gave me a look.

"I suppose my cue is to sell you my agency and duck," he rejoined. "But that's not my style. Don't put any money into cars; the new tariff will smash you. My business is wrecked and I'm broke. On top of everything else, my car was a new model, and on every blasted one sold the valves have stuck and half of 'em have burned up and there's been hell to pay all around. So you and I won't do any business. That is," he added, with an ironic smile, "unless you want to lend me ten thousand francs on no security, to be repaid God knows when!"

"Well, I might do worse'n that," said our friend calmly. Keyes jerked up his head.

"Don't be a fool. I need the loan to keep out of jail, but I wasn't speaking seriously—"

"There's nothing like a good serious talk, sir, says I." With which, the pudgy little man produced a wallet and drew out a sheaf of crisp yellow-and-lavender French bank notes. "There's fifteen thousand francs. If so be as you can use it, sir, you're mortal welcome."

Keyes sat there blinking. Our unknown friend turned his blue eyes on me.

"And where do you come in, sir?" he asked bluntly.

"Me?" I said, recovering from the shock. "I'm looking for a loan, too. Twenty thousand or so. Of course, I have no security; a newspaper man never has security. And I haven't any settled business, and I'm liable to skip out and blow in my money at Monte Carlo. But a loan of twenty thousand would just suit. I've no actual need for the coin, but it gives you a wonderful feeling to have that much money in your pocket all at once."

"Hm!" said our expressionless visitor. "You ain't in love, I 'opes?"

"Love?" I said "Love? Listen: I wouldn't fall in love with the Queen of Sheba herself! I fell for one dame and she was cuckoo. She robbed me of everything I had, fought with everybody I knew, tried to put me in the bughouse, and is headed that way herself. I shook her off legally, and when I take on any more— well, Hank Smith lays off the females, that's all!"

"But there's a mortal lot o' temptation in this wicked world, as the old gent said when 'e 'ired the pretty 'ousemaid." With this observation, our friend dipped into his wallet again. He laid twenty thousand-franc notes on the table and shoved them at me. I felt my eyes bulge.

"There you are, Mr. Smith, and just to even it up, there's five thousand more for Mr. Keyes," he said calmly, and beckoned the hovering waiter to order a bock.

I WAS past speech. My request had been a joke, naturally. I could only conclude that the old chap was a trifle balmy and needed a guardian. Keyes got rid of his shell-shocked look, and then laid his money down like a man.

"This can't go on," he said. "Lord knows I need it, but it looks to me as though you had worse need of a keeper. I don't know you. You never met us before. You can't haul out forty thousand francs and turn it over to absolute strangers—you simply can't! And I'm damned if I'll take advantage of an old man. Take your money and beat it, and look out for confidence men; that's my advice to you. This isn't business."

"Well, sir, I 'ave me own way of doing business." Our friend chuckled wheezily, and sampled his bock appreciatively. "You two gents may be werry bad risks, but I ain't often mistook in a man, if I do say it meself as shouldn't. Suppose you put up that 'ere money. If so be as you don't want it as a loan, then take it as advance payment, so to speak. A bit o' business 'as come up, and not being as young as I was once, I'd be werry glad indeed to 'ave two spry young gents to 'elp me out. There ain't nothing like a 'elping 'and, as the old gent said when 'e took 'is third."

"Oh!" said Keyes, and pocketed the money. "So that's the ticket, eh? All right. I'm in for the game, whatever it is. What do you want to do—kidnap the sultan's wife?"

"Not me, sir," and our friend gave me a look. "And Mr. Smith—'ow about 'im?"

Keyes gave me a grin. "Count him in—eh, Hank?"

"All right." I pocketed my own sheaf of notes. "I'd go to jail for twenty thousand francs any day. Only, I draw the line at getting married." Our visitor chuckled. He produced a knife and a plug of very black tobacco, which he began to whittle into his palm.

"I don't suppose, sir," he said to Keyes, with his confoundedly apologetic air, "as 'ow you've been and picked up any Arabic?"

"Yes," and Tom nodded. "I was fool enough to think I might make good at this game, and I plunged. I can handle the language fairly well, and I've been all over the damned country—regular high-power salesman stuff, getting acquainted everywhere and so forth."

"Then, sir, you know as these 'ere Moors are a werry poor lot o' cattle?"

"Nothing of the sort," said Tom flatly. "They're not Moors, but Arabs, and want to be so called, rightly or wrongly. And the general run is pretty good. I've got some real friends among them, let me tell you."

The other chuckled in his wheezy way, though his blank eyes showed no mirth.

"You'll do, Mr. Keyes, you'll do," he said, pressing the tobacco into his clay pipe. "I was in the ship chandlery business meself at Port Said for some years, and picked up a bit of the lingo, and I 'ave a few friends among the Arabs me own self. Do you know what this 'ere is?"

He leaned forward. On the table-top he drew a triangle with forefinger and spilled beer. He then drew a second triangle across the first, forming the rough design of a star with six points. I knew what it was, and so did Keyes, who responded.

"Of course; that's the sultan's emblem, or royal symbol. The natives call it the Seal of Solomon. It's used a good deal in magic and divination, and so forth."

The other nodded solemnly at us, and held a match to his pipe.

"Werry good. Me name is Solomon, gents—John Solomon, just like that, only me friends make it John—and werry 'appy I am to meet you both. If so be as you could 'elp out for a matter of a fortnight or more with this 'ere business of mine—"

"Sure, glad to do it!" I exclaimed, as he paused. I had begun to like the little old man, and not for his money either. "Look here, Mr. Solomon, I don't really need this loan. Suppose you take it back. I was joking about it—"

"Don't never give back nothing, sir. You be just as 'ard-boiled as a woman lookin' for alimony," and he chuckled. "No, you keep it, Mr. Smith. You may 'ave need of it, says I. And what about that 'elping of me out?"

"Oh, Hank and I are old friends, and we'll hang together, if it's a hanging job," said Tom, with a laugh. "Go on, feller. You've hired two men, and you don't know yet how good they are."

"I ain't so sure but what I do," and the mild blue eyes twinkled for an instant. "This 'ere errand is over at Fez, but it may not end there. It's one o' them things that ain't to be foreseen, as the old gent said when 'e buried 'is second. Suppose you go and pay up them bills, Mr. Keyes, then the both of you come along and join me at the Excelsior, right 'ere at the corner. Come straight up to me room—number four-twenty, it is."

"Right." Keyes glanced at his watch, then rose. "I don't know how to thank you, Mr. Solomon—"

"Make it John, sir."

"John, then. You've pulled me out of a mighty bad hole—"

"I 'opes, sir, as 'ow you and Mr. Smith may pull me out of a 'ole likewise. And if I was you gents, I wouldn't do no talking about 'aving met me. There's a mortal lot of things that ain't to be talked about, as the old gent said when 'e fired the 'ousekeeper."

WE SHOOK hands with our new friend and headed off up the street.

When we got to the next corner by the consulate, I looked at
Tom, and he looked at me, and we came to a stop.

"Is it real?" he said.

"Yeah. It really happened, feller. He's a queer little bird, but
I like him."

"Fair enough; and we're hooked." Keyes laughed. "Personally,
I don't give a hoot! Do you?"

"Not a tinker's hoot," I returned. "Hold on! I just thought of
something."

"What?"

"I only asked him for twenty thousand. What if I'd asked for
fifty thousand?"

"I dunno, Hank. He had more where that came from. What
you going to do with that twenty thousand, anyhow?"

"Save it for him."

"All right. Let's get another drink to celebrate, and then go
see if the *huissier* is waiting to take me to jail."

The *huissier* was there, ahead of time, too, and he passed some
observations on the cash reserves of American millionaires,
and went away with his money. Tom fired his stenographer and
called in a furniture dealer who was waiting for the attachment
to be lifted, and sold off his office junk. Promptly at five o'clock
we locked up the office, turned in the key, and had another drink
on our way back to the Hotel Excelsior. The spanking new hotel
across the alley was not yet open for occupancy. To be frank
about it, I rather expected to get to John Solomon's room and
find that his friends had located him and had him under lock
and key.

I need not have worried, however.

We got by the magnificently attired dragoman at the hotel
door—Tom said he had lived for some years in America—and
without stopping at the desk, crossed on to the stairs. The eleva-
tor was not working, which was to be expected, and we made
our way up past the various floors—the walls were covered with
matting—to what the French called the fourth. It was really

the fifth. Four-twenty proved to be one of the high front rooms overlooking the Place de France, with the city walls and gates opposite. Bidden to enter, we came in to find Solomon sitting over the telephone. He waved a hand at us.

"Sit down, gents, sit down—I 'ave long distance on the wire, and a werry stiff job it is in this danged country—yes, 'ello! Allo, allo, dang it—yes, this is 'im—is this the Dar Jamai? Oh, it's Miss Pontois, is it? All right, miss, this is John Solomon, and werry 'appy I am to 'ear your voice; I'm a-sending over two gents to see you—"

He broke off and listened, then he chuckled wheezily.

"Yes, miss; but it can't be done. Cause why, I'm in Morocco for me 'ealth and I'm all alone except for these 'ere gents, just like that. Wacation it is, miss—what is it I don't understand? Well, miss, werry sorry I am to say it, but I 'ave to take care of me 'ealth, just like that, for the next fortnight or so. You're—what? Is that the truth, miss? Look 'ere, Miss Pontois, your father 'e was a werry good friend o' mine, and I ain't a-going back on you—"

He broke off, and I was astonished to see sweat gathering on his forehead. He turned from the instrument and spoke in an aside.

"Can you reach Fez by tomorrow morning in a good car?"

"You bet," said Keyes.

"All right, miss, you leave it to me," said Solomon, and somehow there was a new tone in his voice—a vibrant, metallic quality that thrilled me. "You sit tight, Miss, and don't trust nobody. Mr. Keyes and Mr. Smith will be there in the morning, and there ain't nothing to worry about. Worry ain't going to 'elp matters, as the old gent said when 'e found the 'ousemaid a-crying into 'er apron. You're safe at the Jamai palace—it's a good 'otel and well watched over. Yes, miss. I'll see to that. Goodby."

He laid the instrument in its rack and mopped the sweat from his face.

"Dang it!" he said mildly. "Dang it!"

"Agreed," I said. "Dang it three times, if you like. What's it all about, John!"

He got out his clay pipe, and made no response until he had shredded some of his cut plug and stuffed the pipe. Keyes grinned at him.

"John, I'll present you with a new meerschaum if you'll let me take that clay pipe over into the Arab quarters and deposit it there. It'll kill off the natives like flies."

Solomon grunted, then lighted his pipe and leaned back in his chair.

"This 'ere is serious, gents," he declared. "I've just 'eard that the daughter of an old friend o' mine is in trouble up at Fez. I've got to lend 'er a hand; cause why, what is a friend for except to be lendin' of a 'and, just like that? Where can you gents get a good car?"

"Well," said Keyes, "I know where there's a good Hispano for rent, and I know where there's a good flivver. Which?"

Solomon waved his pipe. "Dang it! Money ain't no object. Rent the 'Ispano for a month and tell 'em to see me in the morning about it. Take it and go to Fez and see Miss Pontois."

"What's it all about?" I demanded.

"Dang it, I don't know!" exclaimed Solomon with a trace of irritation. "She's been and called me this morning, and again just now. Says as 'ow she's in trouble and afraid of 'er life and so on. She's unearthed some danged mystery and wouldn't talk. It's got something to do with a gent name Maillot."

KEYES, WHO had been sitting on the table, swung off it.

"Maillot? Captain Alfred Maillot?" he said.

"Ever 'ear tell of 'im?" asked Solomon, the blue eyes giving him a sharp glance.

"Lord, yes!" Keyes looked savage. "He's the damnedest rotter in Morocco. Made a fortune after the French occupation, they say, he's in cahoots with a couple of pachas. I heard that Luaytey kicked him out, but after the government changed to civil occupation, he came back. He's in thick with the sultan, he's got a couple of palaces of his own—and the skunk tried to put over a grafting game with me, to supply a couple of cars to the Sultan's gang. If your lady friend is in with that bird, she's in bad, believe me!"

"Well, go get that 'ere car and Mr. Smith will meet you downstairs," said Solomon. "Me and 'im will 'ave a word or two while you're a-getting it."

"All right," said Keyes. "See you later, Hank!"

He swung out, and I met the gaze of Solomon. He swung around and gave me a look that, from anybody else, would have been called hard. I began to wonder if this little blank-faced man with the mild blue eyes did not have something worth while in him, after all.

"Mr. Smith," he observed wheezily, "did you ever 'ear tell of Emperor Ishmael?"

"No," I said.

"Well, if I was you, sir, I'd find out all about 'im—and werry danged quick about it, too! I don't suppose as 'ow you 'ave a gun, sir?"

"No. Tourists don't need such things—and besides, they aren't allowed."

At this he grunted, and went to a suitcase standing open, and picked up a neat automatic pistol that lay on top in full view. He handed this to me.

"Well, 'ere you be, sir, all shipshape. Bein' a newspaper chap, I expect you've looked into administration matters a bit out 'ere—justice, government, socialism, graft and so on?"

I had, and said so. Solomon gave me a blank look and puffed at his pipe.

"Well, I expect as Mr. Keyes is a-waiting, so run along. You'll 'ear from me at the Dar Jamai tomorrow, sir, and 'ere's wishing you good luck. I'm werry much afraid as you'll need it."

And with this dubious blessing, I departed—wondering not a little about Solomon.

CHAPTER II

THE EMPEROR ISHMAEL

THE LEGACY of war has bequeathed excellent roads to Morocco—in some places—and as there are no speed laws and travel is scare compared to our traffic in America, Keyes could let out the Hispano and figure on making Rabat for dinner.

"Well?" he asked, when we were out of town and buzzing north past the farms along the sea. "Is the old boy off his nut?"

"Nope," I said. "He told me to look up Emperor Ishmael— look up all about him, and do it quick. Then he asked if I'd looked into socialism here, the administration of justice, and so forth. I told him I knew all about it, and he said to run along. Rather sarcastic."

Keyes chuckled, swept past a bus that was loaded with Arabs alow and aloft, and waved a cheery hand to them.

"No wonder. Your learning is admirable, Mr. Hank Smith! Justice is administered by the Arab courts; the superior courts, or pacha's tribunals, have a French chap along who runs the show himself. Some on the level, but most of the Arabs not. The French civilians and military hate each other. The Arabs are all for the French, except those that are fighting against 'em. I dunno about graft, but I'll bet I could get by with anything if I had a pull. And there you are."

"More or less what I knew already," I retorted. "But who was Ishmael? Not the chap who built Meknez?"

"The same. The Napoleon and Queen Elizabeth of

Morocco—he died in 1727, left a thousand children or so, and nobody ever found his treasures, which were something enormous, as he'd saved his money for sixty years. He had Scotch blood, or at least a few Irish wives, which amount to the same thing. He was the first black Sultan, and his descendants, who are considerably whiter, still sit on the throne. That's Ishmael in a nutshell. What sort of an errand is this?"

"It doesn't matter," I said. "It's worth thirty-five thousand francs, so why worry? What about this French chap you know so well?"

Keyes grunted. "Maillot? He's no slouch, if you ask me. We don't like each other, and I'd not be surprised if he was behind my being wrecked. Couldn't ever prove it, though. We're looking up a Miss Pontois at the Dar Jamai in Fez—is that right?"

"Suits me," I said. "I stayed a week at the Dar Jamai. It's the best hotel in the world, bar none. I suppose you know that it is an ancient palace which has been converted—"

"I know all about it," said Keyes sharply. "Why are we looking up the lady?"

"We are looking up the lady, Mr. Bones," I rejoined, "in order to lend her the support of our strong right arm or arms. Perhaps your friend Maillot is about to kidnap her to join the sultan's harem—"

"Don't be a fool, Hank," growled Keyes. "We can get to Fez about two in the morning, with this car. Shall we?"

"Not at the Dar Jamai," I said. "The city gates will be closed at midnight, and so will the hotel; and you have the devil of a time getting in, as I learned."

"Where were you after midnight in Fez?" he demanded.

"I was having dinner," I said proudly, "with Kaid Abdesalem and some other boys of the town. A friend of mine got me in—a bird who runs a bank branch there. Named Angel Souzan."

"My Lord!" and Keyes chuckled. "Where did you meet that chap? How?"

"He cashed a check for me," I said. "And we went out and had a drink. I threw a party at the hotel for him and his wife, and we just naturally got friendly."

"Congratulations, then," said Keyes. "He's a prince, and he's one of the few French or other gents in Morocco who has the confidence of the natives. Yeah, I know him well. He's no angel, in spite of his name—"

"I found that out," I said modestly, and Keyes chuckled all the rest of the way into the Rabat. "To tell the truth, Souzen and I and a couple of other friends had experienced a lot of life in Fez, and they were all good scouts, too. No wonder all these Arabs have placid and unworried faces; if the little old severest critic and best friend does any nagging, divorce takes two minutes or less, and there's no alimony graft."

I T W A S only ninety kilometers to Rabat, which is the official capital of Morocco today, and we got in a little before seven. Having plenty of money, we went on to the Transatlantique Hotel, or the "Transat," as this chain of hostelries is universally known, which was located across from the Kasba and the Arab cemetery. It was the beginning of November, and the tourist season was on full swing, so there were plenty of people in the place.

Tom and I got one of the little tables by the window overlooking the street, and proceeded to celebrate. The Transat hotels put up the best French cooking in Morocco, and provide the best champagne, so we were not surprised to see the big central table all fixed up with candles and decorations; evidently somebody was throwing a banquet. We were just at our second glass of bubble water when in they trooped, ten of them, all in evening gowns and uniforms. A batch of officers and officials, obviously.

Only one man was in plain evening dress, and he wore only a couple of decoration ribbons. He was the most striking of the lot, however—a wide-shouldered, handsome man with jet-black hair and eyes and mustache. His face was bronzed, high-boned, vigorous, and as he had the head of the table he was evidently the host. He held a chair for a lady, then glanced around and saw us. He gave Keyes a bow, and a smiling wave of the hand, and sat down.

"Who's your friend?" I asked. "He looks like a cavalry officer."

"Used to be." Keyes gave me a grin. "How do you size him up?"

"Devil with the women. A regular guy, as the saying goes; a good man to have along in a jam. I'd like to know him."

"Look again," said Keyes curtly.

"Well, he'd be a pretty bad actor if he was an enemy—he's got a cruel mouth," I observed. "I suppose you don't like him because he's a handsome devil."

"You're a hell of a character analyst, Hank. That's Alfred Maillot."

"Oh!" I said.

"Just so. I hear he has a regular castle over in the mountains somewhere, and he's in solid with the sultan—acts as official secretary or something of the sort. Some say he's turned Muhammadan; but that's a lie in my opinion. He's hand in glove with the grafting gang—old Pacha Ishmael down at Marrakesh and the concession crowd of business people in Paris, banks and so forth. He's a big man in Morocco, no mistake about that."

I kept an eye on Maillot, but for the life of me I could see no villainous indications in his manner—though I knew Tom Keyes must be right. We were in no hurry, since we had only a couple of hundred kilometers more to cover, and did not want to reach Fez before the gates of the city were opened in the morning. So we loafed along at dinner and went into the lounge for coffee and cigars.

WE HAD no more than got well seated when in came Maillot after us. He walked up to us with a smile and shook hands heartily with Keyes.

"Well, this is a surprise!" he said in French. "I am glad to see you—there is something I want to talk over with you. A friend of mine is thinking about two new cars, and I have suggested your model—"

"No use," said Keyes. "I've closed out my agency. Let me introduce a friend of mine—Mr. Henry Smith, an American journalist. Captain Maillot, Hank."

I encountered a firm grip and a warm smile. Maillot hoped I would like Morocco, and displayed that personal interest which always makes a man liked by his fellows. He wanted to know about my trip, my newspaper work, and everything else; then he turned again to Tom.

"But you are not leaving Morocco, Mr. Keyes?"

"I don't know," said Tom. "I'm just looking around for a bit. Hank, here, wants to see some old books, and we're running up to Fez for a day or so—I'll show him a few things in some of the libraries there."

"Then, by all means, take him to El Wazani's palace—here, I'll give you a card." With this, Maillot fished out a card-case and scribbled on a slip of pasteboard, which he handed Tom. "It's impossible for most foreigners to get into the Dar el Menzeh, you know, but this will work it for you. El Wazani has some remarkable books from the seventh and eighth centuries and will be glad to show 'em to you. Well, all luck to you! We'll meet again, I trust."

Maillot bowed and rejoined his party.

"There you are," I said to Tom. "This bird does his best to be polite and make things pleasant, and you grouse along about how bad he is! Come out of it. Don't be mouldy."

"Never mind your London slang, either," snapped Keyes. "Well, he knows all about you now, that's sure! By the way, had we better give Miss Pontois a ring? The hotels have a quick connection, you know—we can get her on the wire in five minutes."

"Leave her be," I said. "Solomon told her we'd be there. What's your rush? She'll be just another French woman who never learned to use a razor and who never heard of personal hygiene either, and whose friends won't tell her because they don't know any better themselves."

"Huh!" said Tom. "If I had your opinion of women, I'd drown myself."

"If you had my experience of 'em, you would," I retorted. "Why did Solomon tell me to look up all about the Emperor Ishmael?"

"Search me," rejoined Tom. "Hello, there—what's the name?"

The Arab doorman was passing through from the office in the adjoining building, with an envelope, calling some queer name. He came up to us, and I found that Tom had guessed right—the envelope was addressed to him. The man said that it had just been left at the desk by an Arab from the medina, or native city, on whose edge we were. The French occupation very wisely decreed that the French towns should be separate from those of the natives, so that every city in Morocco has its ancient mellah, or Jewish town, its medina or Arab city, and its new French town. The postmen must have a devil of a lot of trouble with their mail.

"That's queer!" Tom passed me the card which had been in the envelope. It bore a line of writing in neat French script.

"Your friend will be at the house of Si Dris el Benouna, Meknez."

Beneath this was the six-pointed star formed of two triangles.

"What d'you make of it?" I asked. "Who's the friend in question?"

Keyes frowned. "Solomon, of course," he returned. "And the old beggar will get into trouble if he uses that emblem as his own—the sultan has a monopoly of it in these parts. Hm! I've heard of this Si Dris chap; he's an Algerian by origin and a *tajer* or banker by profession—quite a fellow by all accounts. Well, shall we be moving?"

"If you like. But how did this card get left here?"

"Solomon telephoned somebody here, or else Si Dris did— don't think for a minute that these Arabs aren't up to date! All right, if you say the word—let's go."

So we left.

The street outside the hotel was full of cars and chauffeurs, most of whom were in military uniform. As we went to our own, Keyes touched my arm and pointed to the car we were passing. On its side was depicted the Seal of Solomon—it was one of the sultan's cars, he said, and probably was that used by Maillot. A little knot of Arabs seemed much interested in us as we got into our car—they were like all the other Arabs in Morocco, enveloped in flowing robes and wearing the usual yellow slippers.

"Know how the yellow slippers started?" said Keyes. "Ishmael chucked the Spaniards out of a few towns they'd been holding, forced the English out of Tangiers, and decreed that all the footgear should be yellow thereafter in token of rejoicing. So it is today. Hi, there! Move!"

The two Arabs in our way moved at the blast of the horn, and we got off.

Even in our short resumption of acquaintance, I had noticed that Tom Keyes did not have the French attitude toward the usual Arabs. Your Frenchman, whether he is a bus driver or a colonist, is a conqueror in the land and knows it—and makes the Arab know it. The luckless native, in fact, gets practically the same treatment as does the Negro in certain sections of the south. Morocco is not a part of France like Algiers, but a separate country; however, the sultan is only a French puppet, and the infidel is here to stay. I had already visited places like the holy city of Mulai Idris, where five or ten years ago not a white man had ever set foot; and with camps all over the country, French towns springing up by magic, and military airplanes buzzing overhead, there is no doubt as to who owns Morocco.

None the less, there are plenty of Arabs who do not love their conquerors, as the present-day fighting in the south still bears witness.

WE FOLLOWED the main highway, Fourteen, and loafed along without hurry, having filled up with gas and oil at Rabat. I liked that town better than any other in Morocco, and said so. Tom sniffed and prated of Marrakesh, which is red and savage despite its palm groves.

"What's up?" exclaimed Tom suddenly. "Is there a car behind us?"

I looked around, startled by his tone. I heard another engine, certainly, but there were no lights on the road; we were winding along the verge of the Marmora forest, with plenty of curves. No lights appeared, but a car with open exhaust roaring was certainly somewhere nearby. It was too dark to see anything. The moon was just coming into full, and was still behind the horizon peaks. Then I caught a glimpse.

"Something back on the road, Tom—"

"Hang on!" he exclaimed. He shut off our lights and engine, and we pitched out across the road-shoulder to a level spot, and halted. Next moment another car came hurtling and roaring down behind us without lights. I heard a sudden yell, a squeal of brakes, then Tom switched on our lights. We saw an Arab leaning out of the side of the dark car, there were quick red flashes, and I heard the crack and whistling smash of bullets. Then the other car was gone.

"Hurt?" asked Tom.

"No. They came close, though—"

Our car leaped. "Take the gun out of my side pocket next you," said Tom. "Give 'em hell and shoot straight. Ready, now! They won't be looking for us to come on their tail."

Both of us realized that this was no accident; each of us knew the other well enough to waste no time on questions or cursing. Inside of two minutes that car was doing seventy and Tom was taking the curves like the proverbial speed demon. I slipped the pistol from his pocket and threw off the safety-catch. We both knew enough about French law to know that if the other chap opens up on you, you can go the limit.

Then, almost without warning, we swept around a wide curve and came upon the other car drawn up at the roadside. It was empty; our headlights picked up an Arab who was running for shelter of the trees. A spat of flame shot from the trees, and another. As we roared past, I emptied the pistol in my hand, saw the running Arab go down—and then we were gone. Presently Tom slowed down his mad pace.

"Any damage?" he asked.

"No. Couple of bullets plunked into the car somewhere."

"Did you see it?"

I nodded. That large six-pointed star on the side panel of the other car had been beyond any mistake.

"Can't be the same car, though," I said. "Those Arabs—"

"The same gang who were hanging around when we left. They took Maillot's car, sure, and came on to get us; that running without lights is typical. Some of these boys are worse actors than any Chicago gunmen. Maillot had found out something."

"I don't believe it," I retorted. "He didn't send 'em after us, if that's the idea."

Keyes grunted disgustedly. "Sure he did. Most likely, that telephone message from Solomon was reported to him; that bird has agents and spies everywhere. Listen, Hank! If that pudgy little old cockney goes up against Maillot, heaven help him! He'll be washed out in no time at all. However, we'll stick with him—eh?"

"You bet," I said. "Got any extra cartridges for this popgun?"

"Nope. You won't need any more tonight; those birds lost out, and will go back home. Say! I wonder what Maillot's game was in sending us to El Waziri? This chap is one of the old families, rich as sin, and has a dream of a palace; he's on the level, too. Anybody would jump at the chance to see his place and his books—I wonder where the dirt comes in?"

"You're too durned suspicious," I said. "Forget it."

I did not share Tom's wild suspicions at all; it was just too unreal. Of course, the veneer of law and order was thin in spots, and anything was possible, but it was usually a matter of impulse. Some of those Arabs might have been drunk and out for a wild time—this was much more likely than the elaborate hypothesis Tom had built up. The Moroccan Arabs live a life to themselves, they deliberately hold aloof from Europeans, and the less mixing the better, from their viewpoint.

"We'll see when we get to Fez in the morning," said Tom, comprehending my thoughts. "If we run into trouble there, you can bet your boots Maillot has reached out after us. Look here—it's only sixty kilometers from Meknez to Fez. Shall we drop in at a Meknez hotel for some sleep?"

"We wouldn't get very much," I rejoined. "It might be better to look up that all-night dance place on the Boulevard de Fez and get us a little exercise and a drink. Then we can go on about daybreak, get landed at the Dar Jamai, and have a shave and an hour's sleep before breakfast. We can't tackle the dame too early, remember."

"You're on!" said Tom with enthusiasm. "I know the place, and we'll probably run into a hot crowd, too."

Despite what had happened that day and night, neither of us took the matter very seriously. Our friend Solomon was an unreal sort of person, and this business of a French woman telephoning for help was not particularly impressive. So we did not hesitate about having a good time on the way.

When we reached Meknez, we had to go clear around the ancient town in order to reach the new French city on the opposite hill. The moon was up high, and Tom stopped twice in order to drink in the view; and no wonder. Meknez by clear moonlight is one of the most provocative sights in the world to the imagination; every detail is softened, and there out of the middle ages rises the city built by the great Ishmael, almost as he left it, with its enormous walls crowning the hillside for miles, and the minarets of fifteen or twenty mosques rising high above all.

And from this we went on to the new French town, passing the camp and parking near the dance hall. This puritanical establishment was patronized mainly by officers—gaudy ones, in their deep blue of aviation, blue and tan and gold and all the rainbow colors of other services. And naturally, officers are lonely in foreign lands, so Meknez has a floating population of interesting ladies, Russians and French and others. Tom and I ran into a crowd of officers and it was nearly five in the morning when we broke away.

However, we did get to Fez eventually.

CHAPTER III

THE JEWELS OF THE SULTAN

O UR PROGRAM went off without a hitch. When the Ban Suisse, the gate just behind the Dar Jamai, was opened, we left the Hispano parked and safely locked, and walked on down the narrow street to the hotel. We got a room, turned in promptly, and at eight-thirty in the morning showed up for breakfast. An hour's sleep, a shave and a bath had fixed us up in good shape.

We came down to the tiled terrace with its fountain and waving poplars, and crossed to the dining-room—a portion of the old palace to which additions had been made. Up above rose the walled hillside with the twelfth-century tombs of the Merinide dynasty; below stretched the triple city of Fez, across the valley and reaching up the opposite hills, with its morning haze of grayish smoke ascending into the sky.

We found the dining room fairly well occupied; parties by auto and bus were getting off, and the hotel was fairly well filled with tourists. We were given a corner table by the front window, overlooking the terraces and the city beyond, and when I caught Tom casting repeated looks at the other corner table opposite, I paid attention.

To tell the truth, I did not blame him. The sole occupant of this table was apparently an English girl; she looked as fresh as a daisy, and coolly capable to boot, and she knew how to get herself up, too. I liked her neat air and the crisp wave of her brown hair, and when she shot a look our way, there was a quiet steadiness in her eye that was good to see.

"You'd better lay off," I told Tom. "You're here to find a French girl that hollers into the phone for help and uses perfume instead of Listerine. That female over there is old enough to take care of herself, too. Done anything yet about finding Miss Pontois?"

"No," said Tom, grinning at me. "But there's the manager coming this way—get him."

I did not need to get him. The polite Frenchman was headed direct for us, and I thought he was going to pass the time of day. He remembered me and gave me a smiling bow as he drew alongside, so I cut in on him.

"Back again, you see! Can you tell us, by the way, if you have a guest named Mlle. Pontois?"

"Oh, but yes, *m'sieu!*" he rejoined, and waved his discreet hand toward the English girl. "She is here, yonder. But I have a message for one M. Keyes."

"*C'est moi,*" responded Tom. The manager laid down an envelope.

"The bearer is awaiting a reply in the office," he said, and departed.

"Listen, Tom—did you get it straight?" I exclaimed. "That English girl over there—"

"Shut up; she's a woman, not a girl," said Tom, frowning. "What's this blasted message, now? Another of our friend Solomon's tricks?"

He tore open the sealed envelope and drew out a sheet of paper, at which he blinked. Then he passed it across to me, with a laugh. It was a notice from the local branch of the Comptoir Auto Marrocaine that an overdue bill of twenty-five hundred francs was badly in need of collection and Mr. Keyes was expected to come immediately and take up his note.

"By glory, I'd forgotten about it!" exclaimed Tom. "How'd these Frenchmen know we were here, eh? Can you beat 'em when it comes to collecting the dinero? Hm! What did I tell you last night, Hank? I bet a dollar Maillot has had a hand in sicking 'em on me!"

"You're crazy," I returned. "Anyhow, the most important thing is that girl over there being Miss Pontois. Who'd have imagined it? Well, you go pay your bill to the collector—"

"He's probably an Arab," said Tom, frowning. "It's not so simple as all that, feller. This company is located over in the new French town—I'd have to go over there."

"Well, you get acquainted with our lady friend, then," I said. "I'll act as Mr. Tom Keyes and go pay the bill for you. I'd like to make sure our Hispano is all right, and get her filled up with gas, too. Suit you?"

"Fine! Here's the money—"

Tom slipped me the notes from his rapidly shrinking roll, which did not matter particularly, as I had Solomon's money almost untouched. In order to reach the new town, I had to go clear around Fez and out on the other side, and I did not intend to hurry about it; so I told Tom that I would be back in an hour or so.

"Meantime," I added, as I rose, "you can console the lady. She doesn't look as though she needed it, but hop on the job and see what it's all about. And, by the way, you'd better take most of my money—I don't intend to go chasing around Fez with twenty thousand francs on my hip."

I handed over my wad and departed.

OUTSIDE THE office I found an Arab waiting for me, and chatting with the hotel guides. He was high-yellow, rather oily, and wore an old brown jellab; he was a young rascal, and spoke fluent French. He turned to me as I came up and a guide indicated me.

"You are M. Keyes?"

"Just so," I returned, and noted his green vest. "You're a sharif, eh—a descendant of the Prophet? Good! Do you ride in my car?"

"I have a car waiting, *m'sieu*," he answered. "At the Bab Bou Jlou. If you will walk that far with me—it is only a few minutes—"

"I know where it is," I said, and reflected swiftly. No cars are allowed in Fez Bali, or Old Fez, for the streets are too narrow; to reach the gate which he named, we would have to walk across the upper end of town. However, the morning was fine; and if Tom's creditors were in such a devilish rush for their money, they might as well pay my taxi fare. So I nodded, and we passed down the stairs to the lower terrace and the street level. In another two minutes we were dodging donkeys and camels and veiled women, on our way through town.

Ali, as he named himself, was a gay young blade in his own estimation, anxious to show off all that he knew about vice in general, and he prattled along in a carefree manner about girls and so forth, as we threaded our way among the morning crowds. Around us reeked that peculiar stench of all Moroccan towns—not an unpleasant odor, if you like sour cold cream, but one which grows on you the more you experience it. Ali was much the same; the farther we went, the more I wanted to smash his yellow face. That he was a sharif amounted to nothing—half the hotel guides are holy men of the same stripe, for descendants of Muhammad litter up the whole Moroccan landscape. Ali seemed to think that the only reason Americans came to Morocco was to get a new line on voluptuous enjoyments.

We got into the Rue du Tala, and a moment later Ali touched iny arm.

"Perhaps," he suggested with a smirk, "*M'sieu* would care to see the jewels of the last sultan? They are close by here; my mother's uncle has them in his keeping, and for five francs would be glad to show them to you. None of the French know where they are, of course, and if the present sultan found out about them—whew!" Ali snicked his hand across his throat significantly. "You are an American, so it is quite safe to show them to you—"

Naturally, I scented a whale of a news story in this suggestion.

"Are they real jewels," I asked, "or the sort that are sold in the bazaars here?"

Ali held up his hands to Allah. "They are jewels, *m'sieu*, which descended from the days of the great Ishmael, and with them is a letter which placed them in the charge of my ancestor, a letter bearing the seal of Ishmael himself!"

"Good enough," I said promptly. "If it won't take too long—"

"Three minutes, *m'sieu*—this way!"

We turned into one of the narrow side alleys, and were instantly in the heart of Fez as it was five or six hundred or more years ago. Most of the houses, indeed, attain nearly this age; the massive iron-studded doors, and the various gates which every midnight divide the different quarters of the city into impassable prisons, speak of the days when sack and plunder were ever-present possibilities. Only a few years ago, in fact, a Berber army was at the gates of Fez, as the shot-holes in the French forts still testify.

In this rabbit-warren Ali stopped and pounded on a door set in the wall. Presently it was opened by a veiled woman, and an interchange of Arabic ensued, then Ali turned to me.

"Enter, *m'sieu*."

I stepped in, and with Ali at my elbow followed the over-stuffed female along a sharply twisting passage. We came into a small open courtyard with a tiled fountain: two Arabs were sitting on a sofa beneath an arch, and they rose at sight of us. Each of them greeted Ali with the usual shoulder-kiss given a sharif, and there was more talk.

"We must go to the room where the things are kept," said Ali to me. "They speak no French, *m'sieu*, but are glad to show you the things."

The two Arabs smiled and nodded at me, and all four of us passed through another door and corridor. We halted before a massive door set flush in the wall. One of the two men threw back an iron bar, then got out a huge key and turned it in the lock, and opened the door. He smiled at me and motioned me to enter.

I STEPPED inside. As I did so, Ali lunged forward, giving me a vicious shove. I staggered under it but just the same, I got my wish—for I caught the rascal a beautiful crack in the face. Then, before I could recover, the door was slammed shut and the bolt shot, and there I was—a prisoner. There was nothing in the room but a stool and a grated window, and a cot.

The calm swiftness of it all, the deliberate smiling deviltry of it, left me dazed.

I stood rubbing my knuckles and looking around. From the window, which was large, I could see only a blank wall eight feet distant; probably a street lay outside. Going close to it, I looked out; there was, indeed, an empty street or alley below, with not a soul in sight, and my prison cell was on the street level.

Since there was nothing else to do, I sat down on the cot and had a smoke as I thought it all over. Clearly, I had fallen into some sort of a trap prepared for Keyes. I was unarmed, but was also unhurt, and since this gang evidently thought they had Tom, the best thing to do was to let them think so and give him a chance to get in his work with Miss Pontois.

Maillot? Possibly. When I thought about that murderous car the previous night, and the clever way this trap had been sprung, there was certainly no accident about it all. In sending us that message at Rabat, our friend Solomon had certainly slipped up.

I suppose that upon finding myself caged in an Arab rat-trap, I should have acted like the prisoners in books, beating at the door and shouting from the window; but in cold reality it takes a pretty desperate or unbalanced character to act in such fashion. I was not particularly worried, and since I actually did not yet know what it was all about. I did not much care. Besides, I was sleepy. So, after looking over the cot and finding it clear of vermin, I stretched out and made up some of the sleep I had lost the previous night.

When I wakened, it was along in the afternoon, as my watch

told me. I sat up, yawning, and looked around to see a bottle of wine and a round loaf of native bread inside the door. What was more, I saw how it had got there—near the bottom of the door was a section a foot long and four inches high set on hinges, and it had been left open after my provisions had been set inside.

I examined it, found that it, like the door, was a good three inches thick, and gave up any prospect of leaving by this channel. The house was an ancient one, and this room had been made for its present purpose—there were several huge iron rings in the wall, much rusted away, where prisoners had probably been confined. Satisfied of this, I attacked the bread and wine and made a satisfactory enough meal.

As I was finishing, voices in French came to me from outside the door. I knelt down and peered through the half-open slit, and saw my friend Ali outside. With him was a slovenly-looking Frenchman; they were lounging against the wall and smoking.

"M. Maillot will arrive tonight, then," said the Frenchman lazily. "And he ordered that the mademoiselle be left alone, eh? I wonder what was found in her room last night."

Ali chuckled. "I can tell you, for I was there," he rejoined. "She was writing letters, in the hotel writing-room, and I went through everything in her room, with Ahmed. We got what we went after, my friend—an envelope with an old document in it."

"Oh, you did!" said the other with evident interest. "And you looked at the document?"

"Of course. Am I a fool?" retorted Ali. "It is in my pocket. Here it is—but say nothing of having seen it."

He passed over an envelope. From it the Frenchman took out a bit of folded parchment or vellum, at which he scowled.

"*Diantre!* But this is in Arabic!"

Ali laughed softly. "Yes. And there is the oval seal of Mulai Ishmael, the sultan who died two hundred years ago. It tells about his treasure."

"What?" Excitement flamed in the bearded face of the greasy

Frenchman. "His treasure? The treasure of Ishmael, which was never found?"

"Exactly," returned Ali languidly. "Shall I translate it for you? Oh, never fear—it will do you no good, nor Captain Maillot either! Still, it is what he wanted us to get. This is a verse, my old one, and you can make anything out of it—"

HE FINISHED with a promised reward which was quite in keeping with his disposition, but which has no place in the writings of Henry Smith. Then he read off what the document said, and Mr. Smith listened attentively.

> My treasure is in my shade—
> Nay, my shade is in my treasure!
> Search for it; despair not!
> Nay, despair—search not.

The Frenchman cursed in disgust.

"There is no meaning to it," he exclaimed, in which I agree heartily. "It is a riddle, a plague, a *poisson d'Avril!*"

"So it would appear," assented the languid Ali. "There is nothing more on the document, and to this riddle, this plague, this what you will, the great Ishmael set his seal! Well, we shall let Pacha Maillot pay his promised reward and then see what he can make of it."

I swung the little slot-door shut. It closed perfectly, and kept out all further sound. Also, it kept all sound in.

It had occurred to me that whatever this thing might mean, I knew at least as much about it as Maillot would know; and this information was valuable. Clearly, Miss Pontois had lost the document, of which she might or might not know the translation. I knew it, and settled the words firmly in my mind.

I was being kept here—the supposed Tom Keyes—in order to await Maillot's arrival sometime tonight; what he wanted Keyes for, was at the moment immaterial. The chief thing was now to get out of here, if possible, and carry my information to Solomon. I was pretty certain that Tom would have taken Miss

Pontois over to Meknez by this time for he had no earthly reason
to worry about my absence, but I must first make sure.

The sight of those rusted rings in the wall had given me an
idea. If solid iron rings would rust in a room, the grating at the
window would probably have rusted a good deal more, being
exposed to the weather. There were no shutters to the window,
and I crossed over to it and examined the grating: It was apparently solid enough, but I saw that at top and bottom, where the
iron was set in cement, the rust was thick—and the grill itself
was by no means solid.

The stool, however, was a good solid one.

There was no one in the street outside. As I swung repeatedly with the stool, the sound of the blows was only a dead and
muffled noise which attracted no attention; and at the third
stroke I could feel the rusted iron giving. Inside of ten minutes
I pulled the grill into the room, laid it on my cot, and had a free
way before me.

It had occurred to me already that there was something odd
about this empty little alley outside, and as I swung out of the
window and dropped into the street, I saw what it was. At the
upper end was a fountain set in a blank wall, and at the lower
end was a gate, and the whole street was not ten yards long. It
was nothing but a passage, probably between two houses; for the
walls on either side were quite blank except for my one window.
And the gate, a huge affair ten feet high, was solid—and locked
by means of mammoth old padlocks.

And there I was, with nothing ahead except to climb the
gate and drop over on the other side—and see what happened.

Which is exactly what I did.

CHAPTER IV

THE SEAL OF ISHMAEL

IT MUST have been startling to the passing Arabs to see a white man rise up over the top of that gate and come down in the street with a thump, but I did not pause to assuage their curiosity. My chief desire was to get away from there. Fortunately, after a twist and a turn I found that I was in the Rue du Tala, one of the few streets in old Fez that a comparative stranger can recognize. I headed back down the incline, along the way I had come.

As it was long past banking hours, which are curious things in Morocco, there was no use in looking up my friend Souzane. My best bet was to head back for the hotel and get out of Fez as quickly as possible, so I made for the hotel on the hillside. It was with undeniable relief that I turned in at the entrance and found myself climbing to the terrace above, among the trees; here I was back where I could take care of myself.

When I got to the terrace, I took a table by the fountain, asked the manager to come out and join me in a drink, and enjoyed two long steins of beer while he explained that Keyes had awaited my return until after lunch, then had departed with Miss Pontois. All of which I had already foreseen.

"What about getting to Meknez, immediately?" I asked. He shrugged and said that I might get a bus somewhere from the other city, or a train from the French town.

"Nothing doing," I rejoined. "I want an automobile, and I want it quick, and I'm willing to pay for it. Do I get it?"

"In ten minutes, *m'sieu,*" he rejoined, and went in to his telephone in the office.

It was probably only my imagination that told me the loafing Arab guides regarded me with curious glances, and I thought with satisfaction about the one fine crack I had given Ali. From my glimpse of him through the slot in the door. I had an idea that his eye was well blacked, and I hoped that it was. These slick young Arabs, with their half-French ways, are by no means so pleasant as the older generation; they have the vices of both races—which is saying a good deal—and apparently the virtues of neither.

The ten minutes passed, and another ten minutes, and a smiling Italian showed up and said my car was ready. I walked back to the Suissa gate with him, and we sent the Fiat hooting for Meknez. Emilio was a tough citizen, but he had a good smile and knew his way around, and he certainly could drive. We got in sight of Meknez before dark, and as we came into the French town we met the Hispano with Keyes at the wheel. Tom saw me, and I paid off Emilio then and there; then Tom and I went across the street and sat down at a table and had a drink.

"Did you pay my bill?" he asked. "I thought you had met up with some of your friends and were probably in the calaboose. Was just starting back to run you down."

"Jail is right," I told him. "So you weren't worried about me, eh?"

"Not a bit," be said cheerfully. "I've been busy."

"With Miss Pontois?"

"More or less. Look here, Hank!" and Tom leaned forward. "Somebody got into her room last night and robbed it."

"Yes?" I said. He nodded, frowning.

"Uh-huh. Solomon's in Meknez, all right, and you'll certainly like this fellow Dris; but it looks as though Maillot had got ahead of us. Jeanne had some sort of a document—"

"Oh!" I said. "Jeanne, is it? And I thought she was English!"

"Well, her mother was," and Tom chuckled. "You don't seem much interested in what it's all about."

"I'm not," I said. "Reason being, I know already. Also, I know what was written on the document and who stole it, and where it is now, and so forth, but I aim to have some dinner before I tell."

"Is that on the level?" exclaimed Keyes, staring at me. "Then hop into the car and we'll be in time for dinner. Hank, you useless devil, I believe you're telling the truth!"

I chuckled and let him pump questions at me, and gave him no satisfaction whatever.

We got across to old Meknez, passing up the Rue Rouamzine and then diving into the heart of the native city. Tom left the car at a garage, and led me up an alley.

"Our friend Dris is over temporarily from Algiers," he said, "and this outfit doesn't belong to him. He took it over, slaves and all, from some chap who owed him money. So don't do any talking in front of the slaves."

"The slaves are emancipated in Morocco," I said solemnly.

"Don't make me laugh, Hank! You know better. Anyhow, here we are; you and I will have the same bedroom with only three walls. Arab style, feller—including dinner."

The rich men of Morocco have learned by sad experience that it does not pay to show your wealth to the world; thus, I was not astonished when we halted at a miserable little old door, which an Arab opened to Tom's knock. We came into a bare passage, which turned at right angles into one of tiles, and so led us into a beautiful old half-ruined palace—a place of cool corridors, courts with fountains open to the stars, glowing electric lights, old carven plasterwork, and tiled walls and floors.

DRIS EL Benouna met us—a handsome man, looking about thirty-five in his white-turbaned fez, with an eye as wide and cruel as that of an eagle, but always laughing, roaring forth jests, carrying out some mimicry in wonderful fashion. He must have been over sixty, for when his fez fell off his hair was stark gray.

"Welcome, welcome!" he exclaimed in French that was almost

as bad as mine, and wrung my hand in a grip like iron. "This is a pleasant surprise—we were about to serve dinner! Another American, eh? Good, good! Can you eat with your fingers? Do you like Arab food? No matter; it's the only kind you'll get here, come along!"

He breezily ushered us across a court and to his own bedroom—a long alcove with a bed at each end, open in the center to the court, with rugs and divans thickly spread across the central space of the alcove. Here we found Solomon, with Miss Pontois, and the five of us settled down in a circle while waddling black women placed the huge round dishes in the center.

Not a word was said about our business; we might have been a casual group of friends, for all that appeared on the surface. Solomon sat pudgy and cross-legged, his blue eyes perfectly blank, and hardly uttered a word all during the meal. There were great dishes of lamb and chickens and other things, out of which we all ate with our fingers, native style, ending with a delicious dry *couscousu*. During dinner, Dris and Tom Keyes kept up a running fire of jokes and stories—and the more I saw of the Algerian, the more I liked him. He could have made a fortune on the stage, with his mimicry and tremendous fund of personality.

When the meal was over, we adjourned to a room opening on the main court, where coffee and the usual Arab mint tea were served. Then Dris took up his position at the arched entrance of the room, lighted a cigaret, and grinned at us. He had magnificent white teeth.

"In the name of Allah! Now let us find out what it is all about."

"And time it is that we did, if I says so meself," observed Solomon, who was whittling tobacco from his black plug. "Miss Pontois, suppose as 'ow you tell us about it. Talk in French, if you like."

The girl nodded coolly. I liked her detached, self-confident manner, and I liked her flashing smile as Tom held a light for her cigaret.

"Well," she said, and from her calm air I had the instant feeling that there was trouble ahead, "my father was French, and you know how French families save old papers. An ancestor of mine was a slave here in Morocco for twenty years. At the time the emperor Ishmael died, in 1727, he was a favorite slave of the old man's, and at Ishmael's death he escaped and got as far as Rabat. There he was caught, but the French consul ransomed him; he was an old man by that time and of no great value, and they let him go home to France. When he got to Rabat, before he was recaptured, he hid in the ancient ruined city of Chella, where there are only vast walls and a few ruined tombs. Among his papers, to which the family paid no great attention, was one signed by Ishmael the emperor just before death. I have lost that paper, and therefore I've no proof of anything, so perhaps we may as well end the talk here and now."

She was half defiant in her attitude, but it changed in a hurry.

"You were writing letters last night, weren't you?" I asked, and she turned and looked at me for a moment.

"What of it?"

"While you were writing, a couple of Arabs sneaked into your room and took the paper. It bore the seal of Ishmael, right enough; and it also bore several lines of Arabic. Do you know what they said?"

"No." Her gray eyes flashed, lighted up suddenly. "Do you, by any chance?"

"Yes." I smiled at her. "Now go ahead with your story. I'll afford the proof."

There was a moment of dead silence in the room. Then she gasped.

"You—you haven't got that—that paper?"

"I don't need it," I said cheerfully. "It wouldn't do us any good if we had it. It won't do Maillot any good. Go on with your story."

She liked this straightforward talk, as though she had been a man; she was that kind.

"All right," she said, and drew a deep breath, and smiled. I read friendship in her eyes. "Do you agree, Mr. Solomon?"

"Yes, miss," said Solomon, and his blue eyes rested placidly upon her, then shifted to me. "We're all friends 'ere, so to speak. But 'ow did you know I was at Casablanca?"

"They have the Casablanca papers at the hotel, and you were listed among the arrivals on the weekly boat from Marseilles, and I called up long distance to see if you were the John Solomon my father had known—and you were. So that's that. Now," and she killed her cigaret with a business-like air, "we'll get back to that ancestor of mine. He said that just before his death Ishmael left a paper for his son, who had not yet arrived at Meknez, telling where his vast treasures were secreted. At least, that was supposedly what was in the paper. When Ishmael died, my ancestor took this paper from the body—he helped the taleb wash the body."

"One minute!" Dris el Benouna leaned forward, a tense and eager look in his face, and his voice struck upon the silence like a bronze bell. "Did he give the name of that doctor of the law in his account?"

"Yes," returned Jeanne Pontois. "I memorized the account, and the names with it. The name of this taleb or priest was Ahmed ben Belkasim."

Without a word, Dris came up as though galvanized, and without even putting on his yellow slippers, went away into the darkness. The girl stared after him, frowning, until Tom spoke.

"Go ahead, Miss Pontois. Si Dris is up to something, but don't wait for him."

"Well," she pursued, "this ancestor of mine could speak Arabic but he could not read it. He thought this paper told where the treasure of Ishmael was hidden. Meantime, he escaped with another slave and started for the coast. This other slave had actually been in the party which had buried the treasure at Ishmael's orders. He was an Englishman, and neither he nor my ancestor trusted each other very much.

"When they were hiding in the ruins of Chella, the Englishman was dying. He had written out the secret of Ishmael's treasure, and he hid it in the Chella ruins before he died. My ancestor found the place, but was captured before he could get out the little box containing the secret; and he never did get it, either. He did not care, because he thought he had the secret, you see."

She broke off for a minute, then made a helpless gesture. "Oh, it all seems too hard to explain, so involved, so intricate! I was wrong to ask you gentlemen to help me in this—I can't expect you to believe me—"

"Don't you take it so 'ard, miss," spoke up Solomon wheezily, as he puffed at his old clay pipe. "We believe you, and it don't matter nohow about that 'ere treasure. The best treasure ain't what you'd expect it to be, as the old gent said when 'e kissed the 'ousemaid. You go ahead, just like that. What I'm interested in is this 'ere Maillot."

Before Miss Pontois could continue, Dris suddenly reappeared from the court. He was carrying a black-bound book, and he plumped down hard on his cushion, shoved his fez over one ear, and grinned at us.

"My friends, here is the chronicle of Zayyani, and now I am going to see what he says in regard to the death of Ishmael," he exclaimed, and thumbed over the pages of the manuscript, which appeared to be beautifully written old script. His hand shot up suddenly into the air. "Ah! Listen to this—'he summoned his son Ahmed—death carried him off—ah! The taleb Abul Abbas Ahmed ben Belkasim el Amiri washed the corpse, and prayers were said—' And there you are, my friends!"

DRIS SHUT the book, and we looked at one another, chuckling over his triumphant and eager expression. Jeanne Pontois stared hard at him for a moment, then flushed a little.

"So that proves what I said, eh? Very well. Three months

ago my father died, and our home was broken up. I had to sell everything. I had often spent hours over these old papers, and with what money came to me, I came here to Morocco hoping that I might find this treasure. It seems silly, I know, yet—well, why not? Stranger things have happened. I brought the document bearing the seal of Ishmael, but I did not dare to show it to anyone or get it translated.

"I went first to Rabat, meaning to visit the Chella ruins and find the little box left there by the Englishman. Captain Maillot was at the hotel, and was very nice to me, but I did not—well, things happened," and she flushed again. "I felt that people were always watching me wherever I went, and so I waited. It may have been foolish of me, but I had the feeling. Then I copied words from the document and asked Arabs what they meant— two or three of them. One of the words proved to be 'treasure.' Another was 'search.' You see, I did not dare show the whole writing to any one person. I was afraid of the Arabs, and I feared the government might seize whatever I found—"

She broke off, and reached for another cigaret.

"Quite right, too," put in Keyes, as he held a light. "The present sultan is the lineal descendant of old Ishmael, and he'd claim anything sure as shooting. What's more, he'd get it, unless somebody got ahead of him. But go ahead."

"That's about all," said the girl quietly. "With that terrible feeling that someone was always watching me, I left Rabat and came over to Fez, hoping to throw it off. I could not. I was certain that I was followed everywhere. And that's all."

"Beggin' your pardon, miss," spoke up Solomon quickly, "but 'ad you said anything about that 'ere treasure to Maillot?"

"I'm afraid I did," she responded. "Nothing definite, however. I asked him about Ishmael's treasures and so forth. He said they were never found."

"Nor were they," struck in Dris. "Listen! Ishmael ruled for sixty years. He was avaricious, grasping, and bled his whole realm to the bone. In that time, he hoarded unheard-of treasures, which were never found. Well! Would I give any of this treasure to our puppet French sultan, if I found it? By Allah, I would not! Ishmael stole it from my ancestors, among others, and if I found it again, I'd keep it!"

"Well, you ain't found it," said Solomon in English, which Dris did not understand. Then, to my astonishment, the pudgy little man broke into fluent Arabic. Keyes gaped at him, and so did Dris, but the Algerian presently nodded as to some question. Solomon turned to Jeanne Pontois. "And, miss, did you 'ave any paper telling where to find that 'ere box in Chella?"

"Only in my head," she responded. "I destroyed the memoir left by my ancestor. Perhaps I should have destroyed the document, too—"

"No," I said. "It won't do anyone any good, that I can see."

This interposition shifted the general attention to me, and Keyes chuckled.

"So Hank Smith steps into the breach, does he? Go on, feller! I'll bet a dollar you're throwing a big bluff."

I sketched what had happened to me that same morning, told of my escape, and then went on to tell of the conversation I had overheard in the corridor, and related what Ali had said about the document. Jeanne Pontois listened with a frown of astonishment.

"Then—it didn't tell anything about the treasure!" she exclaimed in disappointment. "It just gave the riddle, unless Ali kept something back—but no, there was not a great deal of writing on the document—just four short lines, and the round seal of Ishmael—"

Keyes leaned forward and struck in his oar.

"Si Dris, you're a scholar; suppose we reconstruct this document. Evidently it's a rhyming verse, and if you can get a copy of Ishmael's seal in any of your books—"

"By Allah, you are bright at times, for an infidel!" exclaimed Dris with his flashing smile, and he darted off across the court. I looked at John Solomon. He was scraping out his pipe and seemed absorbed in the task.

"Aren't you interested?" I demanded.

"Not a whole lot, sir," he returned calmly. "Looks to me like that 'ere document ain't neither 'ere nor there, so to speak. Miss Pontois, if so be as you and me could 'ave a bit o' talk together, leaving these two gents out of it, I'd be werry much obliged."

We stared at him, then rose.

"You've got your nerve!" grunted Tom. "Come on, Hank, we'll look at the stars."

We strolled out to the fountain in the center of the court, wondering what Solomon and the girl were talking about. Presently Dris showed up, bearing books and writing materials, and then Solomon got to his feet.

"I ain't as young as I was," he said wheezily, "and I'll be gettin' to bed, if you'll 'ave the goodness to excuse me. Mr. Smith, you and me will be takin' a little trip in the morning, just like that. Goodnight, sirs and miss, and 'appy dreams!"

He toddled off, a queer little figure, as though he were supremely uninterested in the matter. The three of us gathered about Dris, who took up a split-reed pen and questioned Miss Pontois, trying various words and combinations. Then, as she recognized the two words which she had herself copied and had translated, he had the clue and soon completed the verse itself.

From one of the books, he obtained a copy of the famous seal of Ishmael. This he rapidly drew in upon the paper, and an exclamation of delight broke from the girl.

"That's it—I believe you have it exactly! Still, it doesn't make sense. 'My shade is in my treasure; nay, my treasure is in my shade!' I don't see what it can mean."

"What about the seal?" suggested Keyes. "Translate it, Dris."

The Algerine did so, putting the translation into French for our benefit. In the center of the seal were the words: "Ishmael, son of the Sharif of the line of Hassan; may Allah render him victorious!" The outer oval bore the inscription: "Princes of the blood of the Prophet, Allah wishes above all things to cleanse you of all evil and to purify you."

There we had the thing complete, or so Jeanne Pontois believed. Certainly none of us could make head or tail of the riddle, if riddle it were—yet there was the document reconstructed which Ishmael had left for his son, presumably to tell him the hiding-place of his treasures.

According to Dris, these must have been so vast as to beggar imagination. Ishmael had not only wrung treasure out of his own people and Jews with relentless tortures, but he had brought whole caravans of gold-dust from the Niger country and had seized the hoards of previous and contemporary rulers. But Dris could make nothing of this riddle.

"Allah upon it!" he cried out angrily. "I believe the only wise man of us all is Solomon Effendi! I shall follow his example and go to bed."

So did we all. Keyes and I shared one of the Arab bedrooms, with three walls and no privacy, and as we undressed, Keys chuckled amusedly.

"Well, Hank, we know what it's all about—and that's all we do know. How did our friend Solomon connect up with Dris, anyhow?"

"Search me," I replied. "Where's he going with me tomorrow?"

"Ask me something easy. I've got an idea that there's more to all this than a hunt for buried treasure, Hank." Tom lowered his voice. "I'll bet you a dollar it's a political game, and a big one."

"I don't give a hang what it is," I said, climbing into bed. "Shell out my twenty thousand francs before you put your pants under the mattress, will you? And did you discover who was doing that shooting at us on the highway, and why?"

Tom grunted. "I asked Solomon about it and he only chuckled, then said to cheer up, that we'd learn to catch bullets in our mouths and spit 'em back before we got through with this job. And darned if I don't believe he meant it!"

If I'd been able to foresee the outcome of my next day's trip, I'd have shared his belief.

CHAPTER V

AN UNFORESEEN EVENT

I WAS UP and out early the next morning, and strolled out in the street, expecting to get a little air before the rest of the party were up and dressed, and ready to depart for Rabat. Everything seemed quiet and there was no hurry to make our departure, so I took my leisure time about getting back to the hotel.

I was just getting ready to turn the corner on my return to the hotel when I heard a shout issuing forth from one of the alleys that led off the street. I started to retrace my steps and investigate when I heard another shout from Tom Keyes, who had run out of the hotel and was making for the garage.

"More of Maillot's dirty stuff," I spoke to myself and ran over to where Tom was going. Then I heard Solomon's voice. "Hassan! Hassan!" I looked back over my shoulder and saw that he was beckoning to a hooded Arab wearing a brown jellab. A squad of soldiers was in the distance behind him.

"What's up?" I blurted out at Tom Keyes. But he didn't answer, instead shook his head and pointed down the street. Then he beat energetically upon the garage doors, which were finally opened by a sleepy Arab.

I dared ask no further questions; but to run up against such happenings left me rather dazed. I got the car filled with gas and oil, and ran her out. Solomon was just coming down the street, Miss Pontois with him, and at their heels an Arab wearing a brown jellab, the hood pulled up over his head—the boy Hassan.

The three of them piled into the rear of the car, Solomon

snapped out the one word "Rabat!" and we were off. Dris was already striding back toward his own house.

"Past the mellah," said Hassan in his clear, soft voice. He spoke excellent French. "To the left at the next corner—that's it! Out past the Berrima gate. Right."

Then he leaned back between Solomon and Jeanne Pontois. She looked white-faced and anxious, but her eyes were gleaming and she was even smiling a little, as we shot out the gate and on to the farther gate beyond, no one molesting us.

"Looks like a lot of soldiers around," I observed. "On our friend's account?"

"Yes, they'll be looking for 'im all right, dang it!" said Solomon. "Now, me lad, what's behind it? Politics?"

"Captain Maillot, I think," said Hassan's voice in reply. "He and my father were enemies. They hoped to get both me and my father in prison and seize all our property."

"Do the French act this way?" I said.

"It was not the French. They will be told that we were plotting against them," said Hassan. "Maillot and the pasha are acting together—with both of us in prison, who could do anything? The French can be fooled easily."

"Stop here—we're out of sight of the gates," said Jeanne Pontois. "He's hurt, you know."

I pulled up at the side of the road. I began to like Jeanne; she was cool, efficient, and knew just what she was doing. She and Hassan got out, and he showed a couple of nasty wounds, which she bandaged very neatly. Then Hassan got in with Solomon, and she joined me in front.

"His father," she said to me in English, "is a powerful man in the south; the idea was to nab father and son while both were in Meknez together. Hassan has been going to a French school there, you see. I don't know what Solomon expects to do; of course, if we help him get away, we'll be responsible—"

"Do you care?" I asked, with a sideways glance. She laughed a little.

"No! And I don't believe Mr. Solomon does, either."

"Right you are, miss!" came the wheezy chuckle of Solomon from behind. "I expect as 'ow we'd better speak French, for 'is benefit." And he continued in French which was considerably better than my own. I began to feel more respect for the pudgy little man. "My son, all eyes will be seeking you ere nightfall; is that not true?"

"All eyes in this land, my father," said Hassan. "Both Arab and French seek rewards."

"Good. You do not know of me?"

"Last night we heard of you, sidi," said the boy. "There is an old man who has made the pilgrimage to Mecca. He was talking with my father last night. He said that in the house of Si Dris el Benouna was a Nazarene named Suleiman, and that he had heard of this man in Port Said when he made the pilgrimage—that this Suleiman was a great wizard and a friend of righteous men. This morning, having nowhere to fly, I came to you."

"You might have done worse," said Solomon. All this while we were speeding along on the paved road to Rabat and meeting no one, since the hour was early. Now Solomon and Hassan talked together in Arabic, and as they talked, Jeanne gave me a look.

"Do you know why we were going to Rabat today?" she asked.

I shrugged. "Things have happened too fast."

"And they're a-going to 'appen faster, if I ain't mistook," said Solomon from behind. "Mr. Smith, this 'ere is a-going to be a werry ticklish game, and if so be as you want to get out of it, I won't blame you."

"Save your breath, John," I said over my shoulder. "Tom and I aren't quitters."

"Werry good, sir."

With occasional correction or help from Hassan, he proceeded to set forth an astonishing story. Some years previously, Maillot had taken lands and a castle—Kasba Helal by name—from Caid el Biskri, and was now confirmed in his ownership. El Biskri had a good deal of influence among the mountain tribes, and like the present sultan, was a direct descendant of the Emperor Ishmael; therefore the French kept a close eye on him. He had now been denounced for alleged conspiracy and plotting, which meant the finish—if they could grab Hassan also.

"Now, miss," and Solomon spoke to Jeanne in English, "this 'ere is nip and tuck. When we planned to get that 'ere little box, I didn't figure on what's been and turned up. It would 'elp us a mortal lot if you'd leave that 'ere box to us, and go slap on to Marrakesh with our friend here, who could drive the car for you."

As he explained, no one would notice Hassan if he acted as chauffeur for Miss Pontois; and it seemed that he would be temporarily safe if he could reach Marrakesh. Now I understood why we were going to Rabat, and it was something of a blow to Jeanne—she had evidently set her heart on finding that little box herself. However, her hesitation was brief.

"Certainly," she said. "I'm to take the car and leave you there?"

"Just like that," said Solomon. "Mr. Keyes is a-going to Marrakesh by train, with Si Dris. You'll find them at the Dar ben Daoud—the House of the Son of David. It's a place I've been and rented. You'll 'ave to drop us like a 'ot cake in Rabat."

"Very well," she agreed quietly, and that was that.

To tell the truth, I was glad we were to lose her; she was altogether too efficient, and made me uneasy. She was nice enough, and pretty sane for a woman, but you never can tell when a female will fly off at a tangent, so when it comes to real work they are better off at home. It is when they get to taking themselves too seriously that trouble begins.

It was about ten o'clock when we came over the hill and saw the buildings of Rabat ahead, with the white structures of Sale gleaming off to the right in the sunlight. We shot across the river, and then Solomon touched me on the shoulder.

"Now, then, Mr. Smith, stop the first taxicab you see and we'll change cars."

There was none in sight, but at a word from Hassan I turned and headed in for the patch of bare ground and ruins where the Tower of Hassan rises—that marvelous minaret of a twelfth-century mosque which is one of the great sights of Morocco. There, sure enough, a couple of taxis stood waiting, so I drew up.

We all got out, Hassan crawled under the wheel, and Miss Pontois got in beside him. Then, with a short farewell, the Hispano shot off, and Solomon and I started toward the taxis. He took my arm and chuckled as he pointed up with his pipe.

"Look at that 'ere tower, Mr. Smith!" he said, pausing. "It's been a-standing 'ere for eight or nine 'undred years—one of the beautiful things of this 'ere wicked world. It's seen kings come and go, and Christian slaves pass by the thousand; and where are they? There it stands, and 'ere we be, you and me; and what's the answer, says I?"

"The answer is," I said, looking up at the beautiful square minaret, "that we think ourselves important, John; but we're like the cactus growing around that tower."

"Right you are, sir; and now let's get a taxi. If I ain't mistook, we're a-going to 'ave some werry sharp work ahead; 'cause why, there'll be someone watching them 'ere Chella ruins to see if we show up."

"I thought you weren't interested in the treasure?" I said.

He chuckled wheezily. "No more am I, sir; but there's a mortal lot o' people in Morocco as are werry much interested in it! What means a lot to others don't mean much to me, as the old gent said when the 'ousemaid sued 'im for breach of promise. But 'ere we be—and now we'll start the ball a-rolling, sir, and a bloody ball it'll be afore we're done."

H E   C L I M B E D   into the taxicab. I told the driver, a hirsute Frenchman, to drive us to the Chella gate and there wait for us, and we started off—we had to go across town.

"There ain't but one thing to do when we get there," said Solomon, who was shredding tobacco into his old clay pipe. "Until I give the word, sir, you keep anyone from bothering of me; then quit. That's all."

We chugged across town, taking the boulevard out past the old walls toward the little private mosque of the sultan. Across the parade ground shone the white palace; I remember half a dozen of the sultan's bodyguard, huge black men in their flaring red uniforms, were having a time of it with two mules hitched to a caisson—the mules were fighting. Then we swept away, back to the gate of the Zaers—the gate in those great crenelated ramparts of the middle ages.

Great as those ramparts had seemed, they were suddenly dwarfed by the tremendous vista of Chella, as it broke upon us ahead, down the rolling ground. That massive Persian gateway is the most impressive thing in Morocco, with its oddly shaped octagonal turrets rising into the sky and the lines of enormous walls running off to right and left—huge, reddish, imposing, and from a little distance apparently uninjured by the centuries.

"Right 'ere the Romans 'ad a city," said Solomon, as we crossed the ravine and drew in under those mighty walls. "Sala Colonia they called it—well, 'ere we be, sir."

We got out, before the gigantic gateway. A mile away on its hill across the valley shone the white government buildings of the Residence. No one seemed to be here. As usual, Chella was empty, deserted.

We entered the gate, took the little turning, and were inside the walls. Here, where had been a vast city, was nothing—absolutely nothing except bare ground. Not even a ruin, except those of the tombs down by the river. Solomon turned to the inner gateway, and halted at the entrance. From his pocket he had produced a folded bit of old yellow vellum. It was blank.

"Now, Mr. Smith, don't you let no one pass," he said warningly.

I laughed. "Nobody's in sight," I said. "Go ahead; you're safe."

He disappeared, and I lighted a cigaret. Yet, oddly enough, I felt a singular sense that we were not alone. When John had spoken about the treasure, something queer had flashed over me—a feeling as though this pudgy little man were about to set in motion some vast force. It made me laugh, yet there it was. And now, as I looked around this amazing emptiness where a vanished city had stood within these enormous walls, I felt a peculiar menace, as though some unseen danger were at my very side.

And then I saw them.

Three Arabs and another in the rumpled khaki of a French native regiment; four men sauntering toward me down the line of ruined walls; whence they had come, I knew not. Casual natives, apparently, for they were talking and laughing as they came. I waited there outside the entry of the tower chamber.

They approached, threw away their cigarets, the soldier heading straight for me, smiling; but I had learned that these smiling Arabs are often deceptive in looks. He came up and motioned for me to get out of his way. I laughed and stepped in front of the entry.

"Go away," he said, halting, and his smile vanished.

"Be careful, soldier," I said. "You do not enter here."

"Is that so?" and he sneered. "Then, by Allah, look out!"

He reached out with a vigorous shove, but I was balanced and ready, and did not intend to hit him more than once if possible. So, as he lunged forward, I evaded his arm, and he met my short-arm jolt beautifully. It took him just over the belt.

He was out of it, but the other three were into me, flapping robes and all; and, if I had entertained any notion that Arabs could not fight, they showed me differently. Two of them got me against the wall while the third tried to get past, but I tripped him and landed my boot in his face. A fist took me under the jaw and staggered me, and with that the soldier came to his feet and jumped in, a knife in his hand.

"All right, Mr. Smith," came John's voice.

I retreated, and they halted in the entrance, as Solomon came and stood beside me. In his hand he was holding what looked to be a little snuffbox of wood.

"Well?" he said in French. "Do you gentlemen want to come in?"

The soldier, who was still groggy with my first punch, flourished his knife.

"We want what you have found here!" he cried out.

"Very well, take it," said Solomon calmly, and held out the box. The soldier took it, the three others peering over his shoulder as he opened it. I saw a paper with writing on it in the box, and turned angrily on Solomon.

"What are you giving it up for? Hang on to it! I'll cover your getaway—"

"Now, now, Mr. Smith—it ain't worth fightin' for, I says," and Solomon held a match to his pipe. He seemed entirely calm and at his ease. "Perhaps you gentlemen would like to see where that box came from? There is no treasure, as I can show you—"

The four Arabs did not know what to make of his placid manner. They glared at us suspiciously, then came into the old tower-chamber with its earthen floor and its walls of ancient earthen bricks. Solomon showed a spot in one corner, four feet above the floor, where was a small hole, with debris scattered on the floor. The soldier went over to it eagerly and explored with his hand. Then he turned, as Solomon puffed at his pipe and addressed him.

"I'll have you arrested for this," he said calmly. "This is robbery."

"Try it, *m'sieu!*" The soldier laughed, as did the other three. "We have not robbed you; we have taken what belongs to our ancestors. But now I think that we might as well rob you and take your money—"

Then he changed countenance suddenly and stepped backward. Solomon's left hand had come up and an automatic was covering all four of them.

"Get out o'ere, Smith!" he said in English. "And do it quick!"

I could not fathom whatever scheme he might have in mind; but luckily, I had learned that he was no fool. I did not stop to ask questions, but walked out of the place. After a moment Solomon joined me. His gun was out of sight, and he was puffing calmly at his pipe as we walked around to the great entrance and so through it into the noonday sunlight.

"Did you get the box back?" I asked. Solomon chuckled wheezily, then lifted his hand and wiped sweat from his eyes.

"No, sir, I didn't," he returned, and caught my arm as I stopped in astonishment. "Come on, get out of 'ere!" he exclaimed. "Touch and go, that was—lucky there wasn't no white man along o' them blighters! Come on, sir, I 'ave a mortal lot o' things on 'and to do."

Well, I gave him up! To let them go with the little box, when he had a gun in his hand, was past my understanding. I was too disgusted to speak.

"Go back to the Hotel Transatlantique," he said to our driver.

"The Transat? Right, *m'sieu.*"

We made the city gates and returned as we had come, past the parade ground before the sultan's palace. Neither of us spoke until we were passing the Gare, and then suddenly Solomon laid his hand on my knee, and I turned to see those placid blue eyes of his twinkling.

"Now, sir, don't take it so 'ard, as the old gent said when 'e kissed the 'ousemaid!" he observed. "Mr. Smith, sir, I've been took and plunged 'ead over 'eels into this 'ere business without no warning, so to speak. I've got none o' me own friends 'ere in Morocco, and I ain't as young as I was. There's you and Mr. Keyes, that 'ere young Hassan, and Miss Pontois—no more—"

"You forget Si Dris," I put in, rather touched by his appeal.

"No, sir, I ain't forgetting of 'im," said John. "But Si Dris ain't a-going to move in the open; not just yet. When 'e gets Mr. Keyes settled in that 'ere palace in Marrakesh, sometime today, Si Dris will be gone for a week or so on an errand for me. And that 'ere Maillot, sir, is a werry dangerous man, just like that! If you and me are alive tomorrow night, sir, we'll be werry lucky."

"Bosh," I returned. "But why go to the hotel? When we were here, a card was delivered to us—"

"Yes, sir, sorry I am to say it, sir, but some o' them gents what was a-going to 'elp me, they got orders to quit, just like that." I fancied that an expression of chagrin flitted across the pudgy, blank features, then was gone. "But, as I was a-going to say— oh, dang it!"

"Well, what's the matter?" I asked, as he broke off suddenly.

"I was just thinking as 'ow Mr. Keyes and Si Dris might 'ave some trouble getting out o' Meknez—but that can't be 'elped now." He leaned forward and spoke quickly in French. "Here, driver! Go to the Bureau des Postes—the main one!"

We swung around a corner and drew up before the post office. Next door was a stationary shop, and here Solomon bought some envelopes. We then went into the post office, where he addressed an envelope to Jeanne at the Marrakesh address; then he sealed it and registered it, and turned to me with a chuckle.

"Do you know what was in that 'ere envelope, sir!"

"Naturally not," I said. "I didn't look. What was it?"

"That, sir, was the blessed old bit o' wellum as was in that 'ere wooden box I found."

"What?" I exclaimed. "But you handed it over to them—"

"Just like that," and he chuckled again. "And on the wellum as I brought with me I wrote a werry different message, sir. We 'ave to gain time, sir—"

"By glory!" I said slowly. "But how did you know the place would be watched?"

"I didn't, but I 'oped it would be. Now let's us go and 'ave luncheon, sir."

We did. And my eyes began to be opened in regard to this pudgy little man beside me.

CHAPTER VI

THE HOLY MAN FROM THE HILLS

WHO KNOWS what might have happened—well, who knows what might have been? Perhaps it was the hot sun on the walls of Chella, perhaps not; but we had barely risen from the luncheon table and crossed into the coffee salon, when Solomon staggered and then collapsed.

I got him to an upstairs room by the little stairway off the salon, and he refused to have a doctor called. He lay there looking up at us, a pitiful little old man.

"It's me 'art—I 'ave these 'ere spells at times," he said faintly. "In me left weskit pocket, sir—the pills—"

I found a tiny vial of nitroglycerin pills. He had an aneurism which came on at times, and in fifteen minutes he was much himself again; but wheezily declared that we must remain here until the morrow at least. Any exertion when one of these attacks was upon him, would only be dangerous and would do no good. I let him sleep, and finding that among the tourist guests there was a doctor from Paris, I asked him about it.

"By all means he must remain here in bed today, *m'sieu*," was the decided response. "No, there is nothing anyone can do in such a case—complete rest is imperative. Tomorrow? Yes, if he feels like it."

As a matter of fact, I discovered later that Solomon had scarcely slept since meeting us in Casablanca; he had been on the go continually, and now he slept the entire afternoon away. And, while he slept, things happened.

I sent Tom Keyes a telegram at the Dar ben Daoud in Marrakesh, trusting it would reach him, explaining the delay and giving our address. Then I went out for a walk, and the first person I met was that same chap Ali who had trapped me in Fez. I was delighted to see that he had a beautiful shiner, and the rascal had the impudence to grin at me insolently as he sauntered past. I came back to the hotel in a thoughtful mood; they had us located, sure enough.

Solomon was sound asleep. I loafed about the patio, got off a couple of letters from the writing room—and was on hand to receive a telegram. When I read it my heart sank:

> "No one has arrived here; the house awaits you.
> Hamet ben Omra."

And there I was, in blank ignorance. Evidently this Hamet was a caretaker who knew that Solomon was to have this palace, and had sense enough to receive telegrams and answer them, which was some comfort. Miss Pontois could not reach Marrakesh before sometime tonight at the earliest, or perhaps tomorrow; I was uncertain as to the distance.

I went into the salon and tried to read the morning papers, but found nothing of interest in them. Then, looking out at the patio and the little entrance, I saw a singular thing. An Arab stalked in at the gate, with two followers; these squatted down and waited, while he went on to the office. He was a wild-looking creature. He wore rags, his head and breast were bare, long hair tumbled about his shoulders, and his sunken, dirty features were lit by two wild gray eyes—nothing strange in a country where half the people are descended from Christian slaves or blond Berbers of the hills.

After a minute the Arab doorman came up to me. He was excited and nervous.

"M'sieu," he said, "there is a man to see M. Suleiman. He is a very holy man from the hills, named Hajj Muhammad—"

"M. Solomon is ill and asleep," I retorted. "Was he that wild animal who just came in?"

"*M'sieu!*" The doorman was horrified. "He is a saint, very holy, and he—"

Just then the saint stalked in and stood looking at me. He spoke in Arabic and held out a small gold ring. The doorman took it and gave it to me.

"He says that M. Suleiman sent this to him from Meknez, *m'sieu.* He says that your friend is not asleep."

"I'll go and see," I said.

On the way upstairs. I examined the ring. It was old and worn, and graven in the face, like a seal, was the symbol of two inter-laced triangles—the Seal of Solomon. I remembered what Tom had said about John getting into trouble if he used this symbol in Morocco, and grunted to myself as I stepped into the room.

I found Solomon awake and looking much like himself.

"There's a wild bird wants to see you, John," I said, and gave him the ring. "Says you sent this to him—"

"Dang it! Not Hajj Muhammad?" Solomon came to one elbow.

"Yes. The doorman says he's a holy man, but—"

"Bring 'im up 'ere, sir, and quick about it!"

John's voice brooked no argument. I went back down and got the saint and the doorman, and they came up to the room. There we found John sitting on the bed. The saint stalked in and gave him the usual salutation, which John returned. Then Hajj Muhammad squatted down on his hunkers and stared at John, who was fumbling with his pipe. The doorman, who was tremendously impressed, told me afterward what was said—it was all in Arabic.

"I have come to look at you," said the holy man abruptly, "and to ask you questions."

"Ask, in the name of Allah!" returned John. "I also have a question to ask you."

"By Allah, I am defiled by sitting in this house of infidels!" and the saint spat on the tiled floor. "Tell me, first, why is man born?"

"By the will of Allah," said Solomon, and the saint grunted at that.

"Why, then, does he die?"

"Because he is a man."

Again the holy man grunted. "What is man, then, the day before his birth?"

Solomon stared at him with his expressionless blue eyes, and the gray eyes of the saint blazed back at him fiercely.

"The day before his birth," said John, "man is as the seed in the hand of the sower."

"And what is he five minutes after death?"

"What Allah wills."

"I see that you are not a fool," said the saint, losing his fierce look. "What desire you of me?"

"There was a man whose mother was widowed," said John slowly. "He sent to the great King Suleiman asking for help. His message—"

"That has nothing to do with me," and Hajj Muhammad came to his feet, but as he did so he made a certain gesture to Solomon, perhaps of caution. "The air of this house stifles me, and it bears the poison of infidels; may it be accursed! Save your questions for another day."

"As you like," returned Solomon. "The Dar ben Daoud in Marrakesh is no house of infidels, but it lacks servants who can be trusted."

The saint showed yellow fangs in a grin.

"Peace be upon you!" he said, and stalked out, with the doorman after him.

"Go down and see what 'appens below," said John to me, and I followed.

Nothing happened, however. The saint walked out, thrust his feet into the slippers he had left at the door, and strode away

with his two ragged followers after him. I stood at the gate to
see if anything took place, but in vain; it was there the doorman,
standing beside me, spoke in an awed voice of what had been
said upstairs, and asked what it all meant. I knew no more than
he, and said so.

Solomon was whittling at his tobacco plug when I came back
into the room, which was red with the sunset light. I told him
about the telegram and asked who this holy rascal was.

"Well, sir," and John chuckled, "these 'ere saints are mostly
mad, but they 'ave an uncommon lot o' power in Morocco. That
'ere gent could walk into any 'ouse or shop from the sultan's
palace down, and do what 'e wanted, and they'd consider it an
honor, just like that!"

"You didn't get far with him," I commented.

"You wait and see," and John chuckled once more. "With that
'ere doorman present, 'e wasn't doing no talking, not 'im! It'll be
all over town inside an hour that 'e was 'ere to see me, and what 'e
said. That's why 'e 'ad the doorman 'ere. But don't you worry, sir;
'im and me understand each other, as the 'ousemaid said when
the old gent up and kissed her."

"Well," I said, "what's the program now?"

"What time is it?"

"Five thirty."

"Dang it, I've got to 'ave money—"

"I have your twenty thousand francs—"

"No, keep it; that 'ere don't count." John filled his pipe and
lighted it. "Hm! Banks are closed, but everything else is open
for another hour or two. Werry good, Mr. Smith, sir, you speak
to the 'otel manager, just like that. If so be as there's a branch of
the Crédit Lyonnais 'ere in town, I want the manager 'ere inside
o' ten minutes; or Barclay's Bank will do, either one."

"Do you think he'll come?" I asked skeptically. "You know
these bank managers—"

"If 'e gets word that unless 'e comes, 'e'll up and lose 'is ruddy
job inside o' two weeks, then you'll see 'im right 'ere to find out

about it," said John. "Get that 'ere message to 'im, sir, and leave 'im to me. Then you pop downtown and buy me some things—dang it, I lost me bag! I want a toothbrush and pajamas and the 'ole blessed works a man needs—"

"All right—no time to waste, then," I said.

I WENT down and located the hotel manager. He listened to what I had to say as though it dazed him, as well it might; the managers of branch banks in Morocco are little tin gods. When he slyly suggested the English bank, I told him to go ahead, and he grinned.

"I will get him, *m'sieu,* and heaven help your friend M. Solomon! This Englishman is a lion, an autocrat, a personage!"

I shrugged and went off about my business. I wanted to get back and see what happened, for I began to be afraid that poor old Solomon was a bit off his head.

However, my purchases took time, and the carriage and pair of horses I employed was no racing equipage. It was well after dark before I had everything Solomon needed, and a few things I needed, and was headed back to the Transat.

When I got there with my two handbags, the hotel manager threw up his hands.

"He is upstairs now, *m'sieu*—and there is another gentleman waiting. Will you see him?"

I would, and I did. He was a Frenchman, and the local agent for Fiat and Renault cars, and he said that he had brought the car M. Solomon had ordered. It was a whopping big Renault, and was sitting right under the salon window. I walked over and looked out, and whistled. There went eighty or ninety thousand francs at one crack—if true.

For a minute I was pretty well knocked out, for it certainly looked as though John were somewhat balmy. Before I could think up what to say, however, down the little stairway into the salon came Solomon himself, and with him an extremely affable Englishman, who shook hands cordially as John introduced us, then nodded to Solomon.

"The cash will be here at nine in the morning, sir," he said. "Meantime, issue any checks you like, and they will be taken care of. If our Marrakesh correspondents can be of service to you, call upon them; I shall write them full instructions in the morning."

That was one miracle, and the next happened when John wrote out a check for the new car and told the scraping and bowing agent to bring it around at nine-thirty in the morning. When we were alone, I looked at John, and he chuckled.

"I 'ave a bit o' brass 'ere and there, sir; don't take it so 'ard," he said. "Dang it, I'll 'ave to go back to bed—me 'eart ain't as good as I thought it was!"

I got him back upstairs, and opened up the bags, and when he had climbed into his new pajamas John went to bed and said not to disturb him for dinner because he wanted to sleep and be in shape by morning. My own room adjoined his.

I got shaved and then was starting downstairs when the doorman said a man wanted to see me. He was a Frenchman, and very apologetic but extremely firm. He said that he wanted me to come along with him to police headquarters and show my passport and whatever papers I had—a mere matter of formality. His card showed him to be a special agent, and he was very polite about it, so I got my papers and accompanied him out to his car, without disturbing Solomon.

Beyond the bother of it, I paid little attention to the matter. More than once I had been called upon by the *Service des Étrangers* to account for myself; visiting journalists who make no secret of their occupation are liable to be looked upon with a jealous eye, for under the surface Morocco is seething with radicalism—the French colonists hate the military, and there are plenty of disaffected elements among the Arabs themselves, as witness the fighting that has been going on for years in the south and east. In certain parts of Morocco, indeed, every automobile must be rigorously accounted for by telegram, and if the tourist neglects to wire ahead so that the police may meet him and give him the once over, then it is just too bad—for him.

Supposing this to be the usual sort of summons, I chatted with my guardian and paid little heed to the surroundings. When we halted, he ushered me into a room where a very slovenly Frenchman with a huge mustache sat at a desk, then left us alone. Trying hard to be impressive, the Frenchman, whose uniform collar bore the Seal of Solomon, showing that he was in the sultan's service, nominally, took up an official paper and glared at me.

"You are M. Smeeth?"

"Yes," I said, and anticipating his request, laid down my passport. He looked through it and then lit a cigaret.

"This does not bear the *'bon Pour Maroc'* visa," he said.

"Which is a dead letter," I commented. "No foreign passport needs it. This was stamped when I came into the country."

"Yes?" He smiled in a nasty way. "It does not show that you have had it okeyed by the Chief de Region anywhere in Maroc. Yet this should have been done within three days of your arrival in each place."

"More nonsense," I said, a little angrily. "You know perfectly well that this isn't necessary with tourists."

"Yes?" He smiled again. "I believe, *m'sieu,* that you drove an automobile from Meknez to Rabat this morning?"

"What of it?" I asked.

"Then you have the required International Touring Card which the law demands of each driver?"

"Now, my friend, listen to me a moment," I said. "I don't know whether you're out for graft, or whether you're just trying to show your authority; and in either case, I don't care. I am a journalist, and as such I'm accustomed to getting rather politely treated by French officials; as such, also, the little bluff of your official position doesn't impress me at all. I've broken your technicalities just as everyone else breaks them, and I'll go right on doing it as everyone else does. And you'd better like it. Since you don't want to be polite, you'll find that I can be as nasty as you can—and perhaps with more result."

An untactful speech, certainly, but I was preparing the way to come around gracefully and slip him the ten-franc note he probably wanted. However, in this I was sadly mistaken.

"Very well, *m'sieu*," he said coldly. "You are under arrest—"

"I'm what?" I cut in. "Look here, I want to see the American consul, and your superior—"

"I regret that neither are available," he said, and looking me in the eyes, smiled again. "It is very sad, but you must wait in jail, until we have investigated matters. Perhaps there will be further charges against you—"

AT THIS moment the door opened. Into the room came a man who wore an aviation helmet and leather coat. He was Captain Maillot, and he went straight to the desk without a glance at me.

"Your pardon, *m'sieu!*" he exclaimed. "I have just landed from Meknez, and there is a matter of the utmost importance—"

Maillot turned, looked at me, and then started in astonishment. A smile came to his face.

"Ah! Why, it is the friend of M. Keyes!" he exclaimed, and put out his hand in frank cordiality. "A pleasant surprise, M.—Smith, is it not?"

"This gentleman," said the official at the desk, "has been guilty of certain infractions of the regulations governing foreigners, M. Maillot. I am about to place him under arrest."

"Nonsense, nonsense!" Maillot's brows shot up, then he winked at me. "I beg of you, my dear fellow, be reasonable! As a favor to me, let us say—a personal favor. I know this gentleman and can vouch for him. Perhaps, if I may have a word with you in private—"

The official rose and, with a nod, stepped outside with Maillot. I stepped forward to the desk to see what kind of a report the mustached frog had on me—and then my eye was caught by two names upon a telegram that lay open. I had time for only one glance; a rattle at the door warned me and I stepped back again as the two re-entered the room. The typed words swam before my eyes and I scarcely heard what was said, for an instant. I can still see the words:

"—Keyes, American, jumped from train, temporarily at liberty. Dris el Benouna, native, killed resisting arrest—"

Just a fragment, no more; but enough to shock me, stun me, set my pulses leaping in hot anger and yet send the cold chill of warning down my spine as well. Keyes and Si Dris must have started for Marrakesh by train, certainly. Merry, laughing Si Dris—

These thoughts, beating and hammering through my brain, were stilled by the voice of Maillot. He was smiling, and it was a cruel smile that sat in his eyes, though not upon his thinly curved lips.

"Suppose we go to my place for dinner, Smith—you're technically under arrest, but this gentleman will waive the matter. Eh?"

Oddly enough, some shade of meaning in his voice gave me warning, awakened my brain to life in a flash, showed me just where I stood. After all—had not his dramatic entry been timed to a nicety? Of course, I was taking part in a very clever little game—technically under arrest, eh? Si Dris had been murdered; poor Tom was a fugitive. Solomon was back there at the hotel, sick and alone.

There were just two things I could do. I might resist and see what happened; or I might play the game and try to use my brains. I chose the latter and wiser course.

"That's very good of you," I rejoined, with a smile. "I'd like to use the telephone, if I may—to let my friend know where I am."

"Oh, the fat little Englishman?" Maillot laughed. "By all means, by all means!"

I took the instrument from its rack on the desk and asked for the Transat, and in a moment had the manager on the wire.

"This is M. Smith," I said, and glanced up to meet Maillot's gaze as I spoke. "Kindly tell M. Solomon—wake him up and tell him—that I am dining with Captain Maillot; and I may not be back."

Maillot's eyes changed, narrowed, rested alertly upon me as I laid down the instrument.

"So!" he exclaimed. "You realize that fact, eh?"

"I'm not a fool," I rejoined, and smiled. "Are we to have a pleasant dinner or not?"

He broke into a short laugh and drew my arm in his—a friendly, cordial gesture.

"Of course, of course!" he said, and waved to the official. *"Au revoir, mon ami!* Come along, my dear M. Smith—ah, you are no fool indeed! Here's my car—"

A two-seater stood by the curb outside, and Maillot took the wheel. As he drove, he chatted amiably of his little establishment here in town, of how he had just come from Meknez by military 'plane, and so forth—still playing the game of having rescued me from arrest. Yet all the while, he knew that I knew the truth. I had had my choice between actual arrest and going with him.

And was it his hand which had struck elsewhere that same day? What madness, what show of force or threat, what utter desperation, had caused the laughing Si Dris to resist to the death, had sent Tom Keyes plunging from a moving train? Well, at least I did not intend to let this smiling Frenchman have his way with me. He was altogether too cocksure of himself, too certain that he held Henry Smith in the hollow of his hand.

We had just passed the new church and were heading for the new quarter of villas, when I twisted around in my seat beside him. No other car was in sight.

"Hold on!" I exclaimed sharply. "Slow down!"

"Eh?" Startled, he peered forward and put on the brakes. "Why?"

"So we won't go off the road, of course," I said, and swung on him.

Not with my fist, of course; it is a hard job, almost an impossibility, to knock out a man in such position, particularly when you are sitting at his left side—foreign cars are usually right-hand drive. But this was a crack old Jimmy Finerty had once shown me; a chopping cut with the edge of the right hand, and if it goes to the exact spot, your man is ready for the finish.

This one went to the spot—right to Maillot's adam's apple. He gave a gurgling gasp and crumpled up sideways. I grabbed for the emergency brake, then turned and hauled off with my left, just as his head jerked up and his hands went spasmodically to his pockets. My fist caught him flush under the angle of his big jaw, and that finished him.

So there we were. I had hooked a big fish—and did not know what in the devil to do with him.

CHAPTER VII

THE BLACK BOX

WHILE I was making up my mind what to do, I made sure of Maillot. I took a gun from his pocket, then took off his leather helmet and used the ear-flaps as a gag, the rest of it hid his face. His wrists I tied behind his back with his own handkerchief, and that made him plenty safe. When I had crowded him over to the other side of the car—which had meantime halted by the curb—I switched off the dash light, then got under the wheel myself. He was invisible except in the full stream of lights from some passing car, and there were few cars abroad at this, the dinner hour.

Turning the car, I headed back whence we had come—one of the residency buildings. I did not know which one it was, but could find it again by the location, and sure enough, there was the entrance. I pulled up and jumped out, striding into the place. My whiskered official was at his desk with no one else about.

"Good evening again!" I said cheerfully. "M. Maillot desires that you let him have the telegram or a copy of it, dealing with one M. Keyes and a native named Dris el Benouni. I suppose you know what one he means."

He grunted and nodded, and shoved the bluish green form at me. With a salute, I took it up and departed, but dared not stop to read it.

Now I had to find my way around the whole of Rabat until I came to the street on the other side of town in which the hotel was situated. Maillot's car was a little Citroen, of no great power or speed, and I wished devoutedly that Solomon had kept his big new Renault close to hand. When I came to the hotel I drove straight on and took the car across the way under the approach to the massive walls of the Kasbah. Here no one was about and it was safe from any molestation.

When I had gone through Maillot's pockets and taken everything, I left the car and strode across to the hotel—and it was real striding, too. When I came into the office, the manager held up both hands.

"*Mon dieu!*" he exclaimed. "*M'sieu,* your friend departed not five minutes ago!"

"Who did?" I said. "Not M. Solomon?"

"But yes! When he got your message he dressed and packed, summoned his car, and departed. He had received a telegram a few moments before your message came—"

"Did he go in his new Renault?" I asked.

Even so; and he had left no message whatever. When I fully comprehended this, I realized that I was hungry, and the best dinner in Morocco was only a few feet distant. I took a chance on Maillot and went into the dining-room and ordered dinner.

Then, at the table, I opened up the telegram. It gave little information except that Tom Keyes had jumped from the train near Temara—a village about twelve kilometres out of Rabat, on the road to Casablanca. Therefore, he and Dris had left Meknez sometime during the morning by train. At Rabat, probably, men had come aboard to search for them—hard to say what had happened. This report by wire had come from Casablanca.

I looked over what I had secured from Maillot's pockets and found nothing of any importance to me except a letter which Maillot had written and placed in his pocket for posting. I tore it open and found it to be a note, like the address, in Arabic; it contained a military pass permitting one Ahmed ben Zair to travel at will through the souaffine zone—evidently one of the "closed" districts where the French exercised strict supervision over everyone. I put it into my pocket, as it might be useful in the future, and went on with my dinner.

"There's no use making a halfway job of this," I reflected. "In for a penny, in for a pound! I'll take a chance. When Maillot was talking about his little establishment, he said it was a secluded villa—and I've got his telephone number and address on this letterhead of his. Hm! Use your brains, Hank Smith, if you have any to use."

I finished the meal quickly, went out to the office, and called up the telephone number on Maillot's letterhead. There was no answer—which was all I wanted to know. Five minutes later I was walking back to the car, where I found Maillot twisting and struggling. I took out his gun and tapped him over the head.

"Keep quiet, now," I told him. "You have a hard night ahead, so rest up."

I started the car and headed straight down the Street of the Consuls, where in ancient days the slave market of the corsairs was held. It was here that Robinson Crusoe had been brought by his pirate captors, for in the old days Rabat was called the New Sale and was the real nest of pirates—and not the town of old Sale across the river, where tourists go. However, this is not a guide book but a story of what happened to Henry Smith, so no more digressions.

Without getting lost more than twice, I finally landed in the Avenue de la Victoire outside the walls, with the Casablanca highway ahead. Maillot's villa was in a little side street here, one of the scattered houses in a new residence subdivision, and when I drew up before it and knew I had the right number, I heaved a sigh of satisfaction. No other house was close by, and there was not a light showing in this one.

When I got Maillot out of the car, I gave him a good brisk shaking up, then started him for the front door. I had his keys ready, and when we got to the door, one of them fitted and we marched in and switched on the lights. The fact that this place was so empty showed clearly enough that he had not aimed to bring me here for dinner—probably he had intended taking me to a very different sort of place.

His drawing-room was handsomely fitted up, with huge Arab stuffed leather seats and very fine old furniture. A little room opening off it contained a flat-topped desk, filing cabinet and typewriter, and obviously served him as office; the telephone was here, too. I pulled a chair up beside the desk, jerked off his gag, and looked into his blazing black eyes.

"Now, my very kind friend." I said coolly, "there's one thing that you are going to get firmly into your thick head—who's the boss around here. But I don't intend to do the job in your style. Turn around and I'll free your wrists."

HE STOPPED spluttering oaths and turned around. I took off the knotted handkerchief—then I swung him around quickly and smashed him in the mouth. He fell into the chair, jumped up, and I knocked him back again.

For all his faults, Maillot was not only game, but he could fight. He landed a kick that staggered me, then he was up and at me.

Luckily, my first crack had left him a bit groggy, and he had not a chance in the world. I hammered him all over the waist-line until he groaned and collapsed in the chair, staring blankly at me with burning eyes of hatred. There was an extension cord to his desk-lamp, which I cut, and used it to lash each ankle to a leg of the chair. Then I put his gun on the desk, and laid the telegram in his lap.

"Now, my good friend," I said, lighting a cigaret, "you take your telephone and get busy. Find out what is being done to locate Keyes, and where he's supposed to be. Speak French and not a word of Arabic, mind! I'd be glad of an excuse to put a bullet into your belly. Be good, and maybe you'll live to fight another day. Go ahead!"

He refused, none too politely, but after he got a tap over the ear with his gun, he gave in and took up the instrument. I sat in his desk-chair and took the extension receiver usually found on French telephones, and listened in. While he talked, I pulled open his desk drawers and looked things over. The very first thing I found was a beautiful ivory-handled revolver fitted with a silencer. I laid this out and grinned at him, and saw his eyes flicker. The thing was loaded and ready for use, and he knew perfectly well that I could shoot him a dozen times over and no one could possibly hear it; with this, I had him where I wanted him.

The papers that came to light were chiefly Arabic. There was a little steel safety-box, which one of his keys opened; this contained a good deal of cash and bank-notes, with odds and ends of jewels and trinkets. I shut it up again and put it away. Presently he laid down the instrument and sank back wearily in his chair.

"Are you satisfied?" he said.

I nodded and rose; going to a tantalus and opening it, I found a nice little stock of liquors, and mixed a whiskey-and-soda. I was entirely satisfied. With morning, searching parties would be out after Tom, but until then, nothing doing; a white man wandering around the country-side had no more chance of hiding out or escaping than would the proverbial snowball in hell. Also, I found that he had jumped from the train when it slowed for the first suspension bridge beyond Temara. So I knew about where Tom was located.

Sitting down at the desk, I enjoyed my drink and looked at Maillot. He was very pale.

"You will suffer for this outrage, you know," he muttered.

"Forget that nonsense," I said. "You didn't find me waiting for you at Fez, eh? Thought Keyes was in the trap, did you? Well, I took his place, and walked out again. Then you went to Meknez and pulled this dirty work on El Biskri. Just why did you have Keyes and Si Dris attacked on the train?"

Maillot wet his lips. "They were not attacked," he said. "They got into a fight with some soldiers and—"

"Try something new," I cut in scornfully. "And the birds you had all planted and ready, cut loose with guns, eh? No wonder Tom jumped for it! I suppose he saw Dris murdered and took the only way out. And tonight you thought you'd pull my leg, eh? Just what information did you expect to get out of me? I might give it to you free, you know."

His eyes darted viciously at me.

"Where is Mlle. Pontois?" he demanded. At this, I laughed.

"She's where you won't find her. And we thought you had a spy system? This is pretty good, Maillot. Now, where's that little box your man took away from Solomon this morning at Chella? Oh, don't look surprised! You had the place watched, and your men jumped us as soon as we'd located the box. Where is it?"

He was, of course, genuinely surprised, for he probably did not yet know that his men had presumably succeeded in their mission at Chella. He said as much; he had just come in from Meknez and the men had not reported to him. The news, however, bucked him up amazingly.

"Let me tell you something, Smith," he said, when I gave him a cigaret and a drink. "You don't know what you're getting into. You and that little old fool of an Englishman! It's a bigger thing than you imagine. You mentioned El Biskri; do you know anything about his son, young Hassan?"

"Never heard of him," I said promptly. "I heard at Meknez this morning about El Biskri."

"You'd better accept my warning, then," he said. "You and your friends are lined up with criminals, with the worst element in Morocco—with disaffected rascals who are rousing all the radical element and trying to effect a revolution."

"Is that so?" I responded easily. "What of it?"

"Prison," he said curtly. "Or a firing squad."

"I'll chance it," I told him. "What about Ishmael's treasure?"

He shrugged at this, but his eyes narrowed on me. And then, in this moment of silence, the front door bell rang. A flash showed in his eyes; he knew who it was, then!

I reached out, pocketed his automatic, and took up the silenced revolver as I rose.

"Be careful, Maillot," I said quietly, looking at him. "Don't make one little mistake, my dear good friend, or you'll be where treasure won't do you a bit of good. That's a promise, and I keep my promises."

He believed me.

I left him there—he was safe enough, even with his hands free—and went to the door. I opened it, and saw two Arabs.

"Enter," I said, and stepped back, the revolver held down at my side, out of their sight. "M. Maillot is in the library."

They walked in and on into the drawing-room. I closed the door and followed. When they came to the study, they saw Maillot sitting there staring at them, and halted.

Just how it happened, I cannot say. To this day I have never been able to understand it, for I can swear that Maillot said not a word, and made no gesture. He knew, indeed, that I was there behind those two Arabs with a gun in my hand. Perhaps they noticed his position, or the one lashed foot which they could see; more likely, they had recognized me straight off; because they were two of the four men who had been at the Chella that same morning.

I came up behind them and was just about to speak when they swung around suddenly, with an outward swing, one on either side of me. Quick? It was done in a flash, without the least warning, and I had only a glimpse of the hooked Moroccan knives, with a razor-edge on the inside of the curve, darting at me.

Only a sideways leap saved me from the first plunging blade; and as I jumped, I fired, and fired again. The Arab on my right sprawled on the floor and rolled over, hitting against the other chap and bringing him down. He was up like a streak, and I covered him.

"Drop your knife," I ordered. "Quick!"

Instead of dropping it, he took the chance that a brave man will sometimes take—of thinking that his opponent will not shoot him down. He lowered his weapon as though obeying me; then it flicked from his hand, straight for me, and he followed it. I warded off the knife with my left arm, getting a nasty cut for my pains, and pulled the trigger. The bullet took him squarely between the eyes, and his hands clawed out for me as he fell, then he lay quiet.

"NICE LITTLE gun you have here, Maillot," I said, covering my excitement with an assumption of coolness which I was far from feeling.

Maillot looked up at me, his hands clenched, and hatred blazed in his face.

"You devil!" he exclaimed.

"You flatter me, my dear good friend," I said, and laughed slightly. "Now you'll have some explaining to do to the authorities; but you can probably wangle it all right. These look like two of the chaps who jumped us at Chella this morning. Let's see if they have the box—eh?"

Anxiety leaped into his battered features, and he leaned forward tensely as I stooped to explore the coarse, filthy garments of the two men. Sure enough, I found it—the same little black box. I held it up.

"Kind of them to bring it back to me, eh?" I said. "If anything's in it—"

I opened it before Maillot's bulging eyes and found the folded piece of vellum wadded into it—the same upon which Solomon had written. I knew that he wanted Maillot to get this, and for a moment I was stumped; then Maillot himself gave me the clue.

"Listen!" he exclaimed hoarsely. "I want the box, Smith. It will do you no good, nor your friends. I'll buy it from you."

I looked at him and laughed. "Buy it—with the money in your desk, which I could take if I were a thief?"

"There's ten thousand francs in that box," he said. "And I have a hundred pounds in Bank of England notes—I'll tell you where they are. Nobody will know. Are you fool enough to pass up such a chance?"

I hesitated, weighing the little black wooden box in my hand. Then I brought the whiskey from the tantalus and poured another drink, thoughtfully, while he watched me intently. This just suited me, but I did not want him to realize it immediately. If he thought that I could be bribed, of course, he would be well fooled as to the real character of Henry Smith—another advantage and perhaps a useful one.

"Hm!" I said, sipping my drink. "There's a distinction between robbing you and taking your money as a free gift, certainly. And, as you say, no one will know. To tell you the truth, Maillot, I think this treasure talk is all rank nonsense. Solomon's a fool about it."

"Anyone can look at him and see that he's a fool," spat out Maillot. "But you're not. What do you say?"

"I'll make a bargain with you," I said slowly. "You write out a statement that I'm using your car with your permission; then I'll run down to Casablanca tonight and leave the car for you at the Societé Auto Hall, that garage on the Boulevard Maréchal Pétain—or I'll have it sent back, if you like."

"Fair enough," he said eagerly. "Tell them to send it back here—they'll know me. Give me the pen over there—"

I got out a sheet of his notepaper and gave him the fountain pen, and he scribbled the statement I pretended to want. Then he told me where the banknotes were hidden, and I got them from a little drawer of the tantalus. I put the wooden box on the desk.

"With your permission," I said ironically, "I'll now fix your hands so you can't take any direct action immediately—put 'em behind you! That's right—"

He cursed viciously at this, but had to do it, and with another bit of the electric cord I fastened his wrists behind the chair-back. Ultimately he could get clear, but not very soon. Then I reloaded the revolver from the box of cartridges in the drawer, pocketed them, and took the bottle of whiskey as well. It was excellent liquor.

"Au revoir, my dear good friend," I said. "Next time you think up a better scheme, when you want to pull one of our gang out of jail. Some of these American tourists are really a pretty tough lot. Pleasant dreams!"

I went out, locking his front door and throwing his keys into the street, then climbed into the two-seater. Not a soul was in sight—the two Arabs had come alone. It was only a little after nine—things had moved pretty rapidly—when I headed past the outer railroad station and came into the Casablanca road.

What with one thing and another, I was feeling pretty good, because by nature I do not like to sit down and let somebody slap my face. Maillot had suffered considerably, both in his pride, his pocketbook, and his person, and the lesson would do him good. And in a way I had taken a bit of payment for the murder of poor old Dris. Of course, Maillot thought he had the whole bag of tricks in that little black box—but I knew him better. Solomon had fooled him there.

Solomon was a pretty clever rascal after all. He had received my telephone message and had read it aright; he had quietly flapped his wings and flown away. A sick man, alone there in the hotel, he would have fallen an easy victim to any trick Maillot pulled on him. With money and a big car and probably a chauffeur as well, John Solomon could take care of himself.

When I reached Temara, I took the wrong fork in the road, but soon discovered it, and got back in the highway; then I slowed up and crawled along at five miles an hour. Tom Keyes had jumped from the train when it slowed for the first suspension bridge—he might have worked back this way after dark, or he might not. There was only a slim chance of my locating him at all, and it all depended on him. However, I figured that after dark he would take a chance of getting somewhere if he saw the lights of a car crawling slowly along or halted. He would be somewhere on the hillsides, or so I hoped.

And sure enough, twenty minutes later appeared a tattered figure holding out its hand—a white man, certainly. I halted the car.

"Pardon, *m'sieu*," came Tom's voice. "I have missed the auto-bus—can you give me a lift toward Casablanca?"

"Who is it that it is?" I growled in a deep bass voice. "Me, I do not like *indigènes!*"

"I am no native, *m'sieu*, but a tourist—an American!" said Tom, showing himself clearly in the headlight glare. And he was a sight—torn, scratched, his clothes in rags. "I have a very sick wife in Casablanca, you comprehend—"

"The hell you say!" and I threw open the door. "Climb in, you big stiff!"

CHAPTER VIII

PREPARATIONS

THERE WAS not a happier man in all Africa than Tom Keyes, when he realized who I was, and got down a good drink of Maillot's whiskey. He needed it, for he was about done up. So we both washed the dust out from around our teeth, and then Tom began to curse Maillot.

It was just as the Frenchman had told me. He and Dris had embarked for Marrakesh by train, and when they left Rabat some soldiers had come into their compartment raising merry cain generally and had picked a fuss. Dris had not wanted to go by train at all, forseeing some such thing as this, and he had warned Tom to be careful; Maillot was not in the army now, but he had pull enough to do anything he wanted, and get anything done. However, the soldiers got pretty raw and Tom lit into them, and a couple of officers showed up and joined the scrap, and by all accounts that train must have been a wreck—when the officers pulled their guns and let fly. They drilled Si Dris and tried to get Tom, but he jerked open the compartment door and jumped.

"Si Dris was a good scout and a good sport, Hank," he said. "And damn it all, I'm going to pay out some of those birds somehow!"

"Account squared," I said, and showed him the silenced revolver.

"Eh? What's happened?"

"Plenty. There's a hot-dog joint ahead—I'll bet you're starved."

He was, and we halted at a road-side canteen, got him some sandwiches and a bottle of wine, and found two police officers, hands on guns, looking us over very hard.

"This car belongs to *m'sieu?*" said one. "He has a permit to drive, also?"

"It doesn't, and I have none," I said cheerfully. "The car belongs to Captain Maillot and we are friends of his, taking it to Casablanca for him. Here is an authorization."

Maillot's note was nothing of the sort, in an official sense, but it got us a salute and an *au revoir*, and we drove on. Tom gulped at his sandwiches and stared at me.

"What's all this?" he demanded. "Maillot's car, and his letter? Real or fake?"

I chuckled and told him everything that had happened at Rabat, which took considerable time. The curiosity of those two police officers showed clearly enough that the roads were being watched already for Tom Keyes, and only Maillot's letter had saved us from questioning. I did not intend to give anyone else a chance at us, if I could help it.

"Well, things look pretty dark, Hank," said Tom gravely, when he had heard my yarn. He was not hurt, except for bruises and scratches, but his clothes were a mess. "What's your next move?"

"Haven't a ghost of an idea," I admitted cheerfully.

"Know where Solomon went?"

"No more than you do. I suppose he went on to Marrakesh."

"A sick man! Not likely. Where's Jeanne?"

"Search me. At Marrakesh or on the way, most likely. She was right cut up over leaving you without a word."

"Oh, was she?" Tom brightened. "Things were messed up at Meknez, and no mistake. Say, Hank, isn't that girl a wonder?"

"No," I said. "She's like all the rest—after somebody's coin. Look what that wife of mine did to me? Trimmed me cold, got all my insurance, her alimony, everything else I had, and has been hollering for more ever since. It was cheap at the price to be rid of her, but good gosh, Tom! They're all alike!"

"See here, Hank," he cut in. "You know good and well Jeanne is no gold-digger—"

"Is that so? Well, isn't she after old Ishmael's treasure? Yeah. Be yourself, feller, and if you want to go praising up any skirt, pick another audience. Where do we go from here?"

"Casablanca, I suppose," said Tom. "I'll pick up my grip there and get into another suit of clothes. Are you going to leave this car at that garage like you told Maillot?"

"Do I look as big a simp as that?" I said. "Not much! He'll have cops waiting for me at that garage, you bet."

"Well, step on it, boy! We want to get there and get out." Tom looked worried. "Let me tell you, feller, Maroc is no place to start gunplay, and this game has got well into the killing stage, and it has me sort of anxious. If Maillot is playing a game that's all open and aboveboard, as he seems to be, then we're done for. Our best bet is to crawl into the U.S. consulate at Casablanca and pull the hole in after us. He'll have every French and Arab cop in the country out after us, and they'll land us in the jug."

"Sure," I said. "But take the chance—suppose his game isn't all open? Then my killing those two Arabs will call his bluff. He won't report it to the police and there won't be any trouble about squaring your case—a thousand francs or so will fix it. Right?"

"Dead right," said Tom. "But it's a hell of a gamble to take, as you'd know if you'd been through Moroccan jails. Personally, I think Maillot told you the truth—that we're all tangled up with a crowd of would-be rebels; this affair of El Biskri seems to prove it. I never heard of your friend Hajj Muhammad, but he's probably some wild hillman who hates the French. Now, if all this is so, and Maillot actually puts the government after us—"

"Do your weeping when the time comes," I said. "The trouble with you is that you've got mixed up with a pretty girl, and you're selling short on everything else—another good sport turned into a pessimist! Get back to normal, Tom. What we want to do is to find Solomon and get down to bed rock—learn what it's all about and why. I'll bet a dollar that with Ismael's treasure on his brain, Maillot will go mighty slow about setting the police on us."

"All right." Tom clapped me on the shoulder. "Head for my hotel in Casablanca, where I left my extra grip and things. We'll get a room—"

"We will not," I said. "Remember, you're wanted just at present! Get your stuff, then we'll go get us a room somewhere else. I've got a mean gash in my left arm that needs attention, too."

THE LITTLE Citroen, which had plenty of gas and oil, hummed along like a bird, and it was barely eleven o'clock when the lights of Casablanca whitened ahead of us. Tom knew the sprawling French town like a book, and guided me to his little hotel in the Rue d'Alger, which had a café underneath. While he went upstairs I dropped in at the café and got a coffee and picked up an evening paper.

I was still sitting there, my coffee untasted, when Tom showed up ten minutes later. He had on a decent suit and hat, and had put his grip in the car.

"Hey, Hank! Wake up!" he exclaimed. "What's the matter?"

I gulped down my coffee and followed him outside.

"Where's the Hotel Majestic?" I asked.

"Near the Transat, in the Rue de Marseille. Want to go there?"

"Sure," I said. "Jeanne's there."

"Eh? How do you know that?"

"Saw it in the paper just now. Early this afternoon that blasted cub Hassan smashed up the Hispano just outside town—probably they stopped for lunch here. Wrecked the car; they had to ram a bus to avoid hitting some fool Arab woman. Nothing said about Hassan. Jeanne was cut by flying glass and badly shaken up, but insisted upon being taken to an hotel room. They put her in the Majestic."

"Good lord!" ejaculated Keyes. "Here, I'll drive. What about that arm of yours?"

"It can wait."

"We'll have to ditch this car first off. I see it has a special license. What we need to do is to drop out of sight, and drop fast."

"I don't believe it," I said. "But suit yourself. I've plenty of money for us both."

"One thing's dead sure—you won't see the paper Solomon got out of that wooden box in a hurry!"

"Why not? I saw him register the letter."

"Sure, addressed to Jeanne at the Dar ben Daoud in Marrakesh, eh? Well, feller, if you ever tried getting a registered letter from a French postman—boy! If she's not there to get it, then it won't be got until she is, and then she'll have to show everything from her birth certificate to her income tax receipt."

When we were a couple of blocks from the hotel, Tom turned the car in at the curb, shut off the lights, and we piled out with his grip, into which I had put the whiskey and silenced revolver. The street was deserted, and five minutes later we walked into the hotel and gave the grip to an Arab doorman.

"We're friends of Mlle. Pontois," I said to the desk clerk. "I understand she is here?"

"But yes, *m'sieu!*" he responded, beaming. "Thanks to the good God that someone has come! She is not badly hurt but she has not been able to talk—the doctor made her sleep. There is a nurse with her. We did not know who were her friends, you comprehend?"

"Well, give us a double room," I said, "and we'll go talk with the nurse. I'll fill out the police card, Tom, while you take up your grip. Then we'll see about Jeanne."

He nodded and departed to the room assigned us, while I filled out the necessary police form in the usual negligent manner—putting down my friend as Tom Jones. If nobody got after us it would not matter, and if they did, we were sunk anyway.

Then Tom was back, and we went to find Jeanne.

We did not see her, but we did see a very efficient "garde-malade"—a trim French nurse who sat down with us, had a smoke, and assured us cheerfully that mademoiselle would be out of bed in the morning. Her injuries were by no means so severe as alleged in the newspaper. Her hands and arms were badly cut by glass and she had received a rather bad shaking-up, but nothing more serious; she was sound asleep and was not to be disturbed. The nurse knew nothing about Hassan. She put a bandage on my cut arm and never asked for any explanation, either.

We arranged with her to have Jeanne ready to travel at nine in the morning, and departed.

"NINE IN the morning, huh?" said Keyes, as we made ready for bed. "You're an optimist, Hank. At nine a.m. we'll be talking to the judge."

"Forget it," I told him. "You know the ropes in this town, so you pop out early and get hold of a car. I'm dead sure we'll find Solomon at Marrakesh."

Keyes grunted skeptically, but I was asleep before he turned in. He wakened me at eight and was gone with the comment that we were still alive. I think he had expected the police to walk in on us at any time, but I was confident of the contrary. Now that I had definitely found Maillot to be as bad as Keyes had made him out, he loomed up before me as a crafty rascal who was out to feather his own nest at all costs; and I felt certain that as long as he had any hopes of landing Ishmael's treasure, he would keep under cover so far as was possible. Perhaps this, too, had been Solomon's idea. I had gathered that the pudgy little cockney was desperately sparring for time—as he admitted to me, he had been pitched into this thing unawares. Well, I had certainly gained a little time for all concerned by my encounter with Maillot. The handsome Frenchman would be in no shape for active business in the next day or so.

I got breakfast in the dining-room, for the Majestic was accustomed to eccentric foreigners who needed a whole meal in the morning instead of the usual coffee and rolls, and in the middle of it Tom Keyes came in and joined me. He looked more cheerful.

"All set, Hank. A good comfortable Delage will be here at nine, with a driver. It's two hundred and forty kilos to Marrakesh; we'll get in sometime this afternoon, with luck. But this outfit costs money."

"I'll split my winnings with you," I said, and got out what I had looted from Maillot, and we divided it.

We went up to Jeanne's room, found her dressed and packed, and had a joyful reunion—at least, she and Keyes did. I could see right off that Tom Keyes was done for, and no wonder either; Jeanne was a pretty fine girl. However, she did not interest me. So I paid off the nurse and settled the doctor's bill, squared up with the hotel, and in ten minutes we were off for Marrakesh. Keyes and Jeanne, who was pale and had her arms bandaged, occupied the rear of the car, which was a large brougham, and I sat in front with Emile, the chauffeur. We were three tourists seeing Morocco, and out for a grand time. The Hispano was wrecked and in a garage. Hassan had vanished, and we had nothing to worry us. So far as Maillot was concerned, I was obviously correct—we had won the gamble, and Tom Keyes need not lose any sleep over the police searching for him.

We got an early lunch at El Kemisset and whirled on through vast plains and into the hills, following the railroad most of the way; and early in the afternoon burst upon us the glorious view of Marrakesh ahead and below, with the showy peaks of the Atlas in the background. There were the thousand-year-old walls, the vast date-palm groves outside, the long huddle of white houses and palaces, and rising over all the enormous minaret of the Koutoubia mosque, topped by the three huge silver balls, part of El Mansur's spoil when he conquered Spain.

"The Koutoubia yonder, *m'sieu*," said Emile, jogging my elbow as he started the car down the hill, "was built by the same architect who built the Giralda of Seville."

"Thank you," I said solemnly. "Do you know where the Dar ben Daoud is?"

He shrugged. "There are plenty of palaces in Marrakesh, *m'sieu;* you go to the hotel?"

"No. To the Dar ben Daoud. At least, we'll go there first, so you'd better locate it."

We ran through the wide avenues of the French town, and so on to the vast circuit of ominous reddish walls which we entered at the Dukala gate, passing on down the street by the Transat hotel. Here Emile halted to get directions, then took us on into the heart of the ancient city, where the railroad meets all the commerce of western Africa and the Sahara. He came to rest before an inconspicuous doorway where an Arab stood loafing. I leaned out and asked if this were the Dar ben Daoud, and it was.

"Do you know whether a M. Solomon is here?" I demanded. The Arab looked me over.

"I do not know, *m'sieu*," he said. "I will inquire."

He disappeared, calling someone else. Presently he returned, and two other Arabs were with him. All three were wild-looking fellows, and one of them was red-haired.

"You and your friends are expected, *m'sieu*," he said, with a grin. "M. Solomon is here."

We unloaded and paid off Emile, and followed the red-haired Arab inside. There was the usual right-angled entrance, then we came abruptly upon a square courtyard with a pool in the center and flowers everywhere: this was surrounded by a colonnade of delicate marble arches. We turned to the left, entered by a door at the corner, and found ourselves in a large, high-ceiled room, magnificently decorated with tiles and the cut-and-colored plaster work of a past generation. Rugs and cushions strewed the floor. At one end of the room was a large table where an Arab secretary was waiting; and seated on a large divan, greeting us with a cheery wave of his clay pipe as he rose, was our friend Solomon.

He dismissed the Arab and came to meet us.

"Werry sorry I am to see as you're 'urt, Miss Pontois!" he exclaimed wheezily. "I only 'eard about it last night when I got word from Hassan, and I called up the Majestic and found as Mr. Smith was there; so it was all right. Make yourself to 'ome, miss—no great 'arm done, I 'opes?"

"Nothing but some cuts and a bad case of nerves, thanks," and the girl laughed as she sank down on the divan. "Hassan is all right, then?"

"Yes, miss; we'll see 'im 'ere this werry afternoon," said Solomon.

"You got here last night?" I asked him. He gave me a look and chuckled.

"Yes, sir. I got me new car and come right along, and 'ere I be, all shipshape and ready to 'ave a good sharp talk. Would you like to rest up a bit, miss, before we get down to business?"

"Mercy, no!" Jeanne took a cigaret from the tabouret at her elbow. "I'm quite all right. I can use my fingers and my tongue, and these pillows are perfectly delicious to sink into! So go right ahead."

"Werry good, ma'am." Solomon resumed his seat and held a match to his pipe. "There's a mortal lot to go into."

"I'm glad you read the implied warning in my message and skipped out," I said.

"I ain't often mistook in such things, sir, as the old gent said when 'e kissed the pretty 'ousemaid. I thought as 'ow you could 'andle that 'ere Maillot. Now, suppose we get things cleared up; 'cause why, I 'ave some werry important wisitors a-coming 'ere this afternoon. You take the floor, Mr. Smith—we'll 'ave some drinks fetched in right off."

AN ARAB fetched in a tray, and we set in to have the clearing-up that was so sadly needed by us all. Solomon assured us that we could speak perfectly freely; he had four native men and two women on the place, arrived only this morning—and all were Berbers, sent to him by the wild saint, Hajj Muhammad. What was more, Muhammad himself was coming this afternoon, and with him several other gentlemen from the hill-country.

"And what's more," added Solomon, his blue eyes twinkling, "they all 'ave a price on their 'eads, too! Werry interesting session, it will be. But you move ahead, Mr. Smith."

I moved ahead, and Tom chipped in at the right moment, telling all that had happened the previous day. Solomon sat puffing at his clay pipe, and very ridiculous he looked, with his Basque beret cocked over one ear and wisps of grey hair sticking out around the edge. His round features remained absolutely blank, even at mention of Dris, and his placid blue eyes were devoid of all expression. I had come to realize, however, that behind this odd exterior were some startling brains.

"Werry good," said Solomon, when we had told all our story. "Mr. Smith, you look out for yourself; that 'ere Maillot will be after you proper. You took 'im by surprise last night, and werry lucky you did—but 'e ain't nobody's fool, sor. Now, Miss Pontois, I expect as 'ow you want to know what was in that 'ere wooden box. Well, 'ere it is, let's get this 'ere treasure business settled and then go on to more important things."

He handed Jeanne a bit of old and tattered vellum upon which the English writing was black and perfectly readable; and I smiled to myself as I remembered what I had thought about this writing. Jeanne passed it on to Keyes and me. The message was curt and explicit.

"Wee have hidde Semain's monies in ye grot yt is under ye French sun dile in ye palace garden 2 wains of coin Wm Hearne."

I looked up at Solomon. "What did you write on the bit of vellum Maillot has now?"

"The werry same thing, sir, two wagon-loads and all—only I put it in a corner of the women's palace, just like that. Let 'im find it if 'e can!"

"Well," spoke up Tom Keyes, "is there any chance that slaves would have been so employed?"

"It's the werry thing as proves itself true, sir," answered Solomon. "I've been a-looking into this 'ere business; we know o' two just such occasions in Moroccan 'istory, one under Ishmael's brother, one under 'is son Zidan, when slaves up and saved their lives by telling where they 'ad 'id treasure for their masters. And Semain was the name them 'ere slaves used for Ishmael. Yes, sir, this 'ere paper proves itself, it does that, and I expect the treasure is right there; but we can't go and look, so to speak. It 'as to be 'andled proper, all shipshape and Bristol fashion."

"All right," I said. "Grotto or cave under the sun dial in Ishmael's palace—that means Meknez. And that means authority to dig. Let's burn that vellum, first."

"Right you are, sir," said Solomon. I struck a match. The vellum curled up like a tortured snake and finally turned into a twisted black char. It made a frightful stink, too.

"Clever of old Ishmael!" observed Keyes. "That riddle— remember? 'My shade is in my treasure and my treasure in my shade,' with the treasure down below the sun dial all the while!"

Solomon waved his pipe and looked at Jeanne.

"Miss, this 'ere will take time. Now, what share o' that 'ere treasure will satisfy you?"

"What do you think?" she demanded, smiling. "You mean you'll have to pull wires and promise a few bribes and so forth, before you can get permission?"

Solomon nodded. "All o' that, miss. The sultan 'as to be fixed, and so do the French."

"I'm in your hands, John," said Jeanne. "I'll agree to anything you do."

"Werry good; I'll 'old you to that 'ere bargain, miss. If we—"

"Hold on," said Keyes, leaning forward on his cushions. "If this game is to be played out in Meknez, why are we down here in Marrakesh?"

"I'm a-coming to that, sir," said Solomon, "and a werry ticklish business it is. This 'ere treasure is mixed up with something a mortal lot bigger, just like that. Now, miss, werry sorry I am to say it, but these 'ere Arabs don't want no women a-mixing in their business, and if I was you, I'd go to me room and rest up a bit until dinner time. Then we can tell you all about it. I'll 'ave one o' the women take care of you."

Jeanne nodded understanding, and at Solomon's call an Arab entered, then departed. A moment later, a woman appeared—a tall, unveiled, fine-looking woman with blue tribal marks tattooed on brow and cheeks and chin. Solomon spoke to her, and she smiled and beckoned Jeanne.

"Now, gents," said John to me and Keyes, "this 'ere situation is getting serious, as the old gent said when the 'ousemaid sued 'im for breach 'o promise. Let's 'ave it straight afore them Arabs come. Mr. Keyes, you and Mr. Smith look over that map on the table and I'll do me best to show you what's up."

We got the map spread out—a large-scale map of southern Morocco—and then we heard something that brought us up all standing.

CHAPTER IX

THE PROPHECY

"ME FRIENDS," said Solomon, as he scraped his clay pipe, "there's a 'undred and seventy thousand Arabs 'ere in Marrakesh; and outside o' troops, there's five thousand Europeans. Inside o' thirty days them 'ere five thousand will be corpses, just like that."

In this calm utterance there was something incredible, something beyond comprehension; it grew upon us slowly, with gathering reality. The quiet, wheezy voice had fallen silent, yet it lingered in the room like the aftertones of a bronze bell—a hundred and seventy thousand Arabs, five thousand Europeans!

"Yes, sir," Solomon eyed his pipe critically, blew through it, then his expressionless blue eyes settled upon us. "Fez 'as a bit over four thousand Europeans, with a 'undred and twenty thousand Arabs. You think o' them 'ere figures, gents: werry interesting they be. Or look at Mazagan, what 'as two thousand Europeans and eighteen thousand Arabs. Or Safi, with fifteen 'undred Europeans and twenty-seven thousand Arabs—"

"Nonsense, John, nonsense!" Keyes wakened with a start and a laugh. "Are you talking about a possible revolt—here in Morocco? That's plain nonsense. The Arabs know better. Even if it were possible, every city has a French garrison, a camp outside the walls!"

"Well, sir," and John Solomon chuckled, *"why"* as every Arab city a French camp outside its walls? You stop and think over that for a minute. It's me what 'as the last word this time, as the old gent said when 'e buried 'is second!"

And he was right. Keyes frowned and said nothing.

Now, for several weeks I had been poking my nose into odd places around Morocco, talking with colonists and French and Arabs, and I had uncovered a whole lot of things. Any talk about revolution seemed utterly preposterous—but was it? There was a tremendous lot of disaffection in the country. Men were crawling in from the hills to die of hunger around the tombs of their saints—this had happened in Rabat itself, the grand new capital.

"Well, Mr. Smith," said Solomon, "are you a-going to say as it's impossible, too?"

"I'm from Chillicothe, Missouri, John. Go ahead and show me; my ears are pinned back."

Solomon grunted as though pleased, and got out his plug of tobacco and his knife. Then he cut loose with some staggering information—if true.

Oddly enough, it did not surprise me as much as it did Tom Keyes, because it was no new thing to me. The country was now under civil rule, but the preceding military government had aroused much hatred even in French hearts. I had heard colonists swear that the war with Abdel Krim had been deliberately promoted by the military to keep the army occupied, and that the French had kept Krim supplied with munitions—active service pay, wound stripes, service stripes, promotion! Truth it was that the civil government had ended that war in sixty days. Solomon went over all this, and a dozen more things, chiefly the attitude of the great caids.

Then he went into religion and recent history. The whole south of the country was a zone of insecurity even now. Fifty miles from Marrakesh the guns were booming and the Atlas mountains was alive to the roar of military planes. The veneer of conquest was thin; the Gueliz hill, which overlooked Marrakesh itself, was a solid system of batteries designed to overawe the city. The fanatical Berbers and hill tribes were ripe for revolt at any moment from south to north. The caids were at each other's throats. The French backed them, and they exerted a worse oppression over the natives, in consequence, than ever before. The puppet sultan was not acknowledged by half his subjects—there were plenty of other pretenders to his throne.

The amazing thinness of the veneer was shown by the fact that up north at the holy city of Mulai Idris, in the very heart of the French power, no tourists were allowed abroad after dark.

"Now, gents, you look at that 'ere map," concluded Solomon. "The military ain't in control no more, remember; their big men ain't 'ere now. All the fighting is concentrated between Marrakesh and the Sahara. Down there in the mountains is pretty near the 'ole effective French army, and the camps are stripped to keep 'em supplied. They're seventy mile deep in them 'ere mountains. And it was right there, about ten mile deep, that the Emperor Ishmael took in an army o' sixty thousand trained troops—and he only got out wi' two thousand of 'em. Now, then, what would 'appen if there was a sudden uprising, if the mountain passes were blocked and the roads cut, and if the towns all over Morocco were to come to life? They'd 'ave the country in their 'ands in no time—and the army bottled up in them 'ere mountains."

"Not a bit of it," objected Tom Keyes. "From a practical standpoint—who'd do it and why?"

SOLOMON LIGHTED his pipe, sighed wheezily, and went on to paint an alarming picture of what might happen if any of the numerous pretenders to the throne started a real revolt and enlisted the fanaticism of the Arabs to his standard. All over Morocco was an endless surge of natives in movement—pilgrims by the thousand to various shrines and cities, ready to rise on a certain day, massacre right and left, seize the military camps and the vast dumps of munitions and supplies—some of which were almost unguarded, as I had seen for myself at Taza. And what would be the result?

"It'd be plain hell—for a while," admitted Keyes. "The Indian mutiny all over again."

"Right you are, sir. And—"

"Hold on," I cut in. "What about arms and supplies and money for such a revolt?"

Solomon's blue eyes twinkled slightly.

"You've 'it it first crack, sir," he said calmly. "This 'ere revolt would throw out the civil administration, just like that. The military would come back into power. There'd be no end o' fighting and so forth. Now, if there was certain Frenchmen willing to back all this 'ere deviltry in a quiet way, so to speak—"

"No Frenchman would do it," snapped Keyes. Solomon cocked his head on one side and surveyed him blandly.

"Dang it, you're a werry 'ard person to conwince, Mr. Keyes! Guns can be run in all the while, and are bein' run in, just like that. Did you ever 'ear o' the Societé Agricole in Casablanca?"

"Eh?" Keyes frowned. "Sure. They're a big French importing firm—farm machinery, tractors, and so forth. American, mostly. They've got a big establishment, warehouse, parts, repairs."

"Werry good, sir. And in that 'ere warehouse at this werry blessed minute there's two 'undred machine guns, a thousand automatic rifles, and ammunition to go with 'em, waiting for shipment upcountry."

This was a bomb and no mistake. Keyes was thunderstruck.

"John, are you certain of this?" I asked. "How do you know? Do the police know?"

Solomon regarded me blankly. "Them as asks questions gets less'n they asks, says I. No, sir, the police don't know, but I do. And who owns the control o' that 'ere Societé Agricole?"

"I don't know," said Keyes. "Do you?"

"Yes, sir—"

At this instant the red-haired Berber came in and held open the door. Into the room stalked our wild-eyed friend Hajj Muhammad, and with him five other Arabs or Berbers—

bearded, smiling men. The saint halted, lifted his hand, and barked out a greeting. Solomon returned it, and then beckoned to the red-headed Arab, who remained at his side.

"We will talk in French, chiefly, for your benefit," said John to us. "Ali here will interpret all that is said. Ali, say that these two men are my friends. Say that this man with the gray eyes was with Si Dris el Benouni when he was killed on the train; this tall American last night slew two men in the house of Maillot, and left Maillot tied in his chair after robbing him and beating him."

I was startled by this, but at once the eyes of the six visitors went to me, and their smiles passed into quatters of approbation; Maillot had no friends here, evidently. Solomon turned to us, the suspicious eyes of the hillmen following his every move.

"These five men," he said, so that the interpreter would miss no word, "are mountain chiefs or leaders of the tribes, and I think all of them are fugitives. Ah! There's Hassan now."

Into the room came the slim form of the boy Hassan. He smiled at us, and then greeted the six Arabs, who kissed his shoulder respectfully—he was a descendant of the prophet. Whether he had just reached Marrakesh, or had been here in the house, did not appear.

The doors were closed, after trays of refreshments were brought in, and the saint introduced his companions in a long singsong recital of titles and so forth—a regular "began" Chapter. They studied Solomon, and so did I, for now I began to glimpse the little man as he really was. I say "began" advisedly, for as yet I was far from comprehending his actual position here.

If I was looking for the point of contact between Solomon and these Arabs, I soon had it; and with it a chapter from Solomon's past life, or more strictly allusions to one, into which I never probed any deeper. I had already learned that he had once been established at Port Said and was known among eastern Arabs, but now came more definite hints, as Hajj Muhammad struck into the reasons for his presence, and the red-haired interpreter kept up a running murmur at our elbows.

"We have heard of you, Sidi Suleiman," said the wild-eyed fanatic. "I have heard of you at Mecca and elsewhere; others who have made the pilgrimage have heard of you. We know that the emirs of Arabia are your friends, and that in your hands is the ancient Seal of Suleiman, on whom be blessings! We know that you have great power of magic and can foretell the future, and when I received word two weeks ago that you desired to meet me, I was glad."

Keyes gave me a glance. Two weeks ago! How long had Solomon been at work down here? Had he really been pitched unexpectedly into this business, or had he been engaged in it for some time—and suddenly found it to be of serious and immediate importance? Hard to say. There was a lot more to him than appeared on the surface. Now he made answer, talking partly in French, partly in Arabic.

"I have desired to talk with you, that is true, and meantime the son of El Biskri has placed himself under my protection. I wish to find out why he and these other chiefs are not fugitives from the law."

"For what reason?" spat out Muhammad. "Do you wish to help us against the French?"

"As Allah liveth, I desire to help you," said Solomon. "Whether against the French or not, remains to be seen. It is in my mind that your grievance is against the sultan."

"May his name be accursed!" cried the saint angrily. "May the air that he breathes be poison unto him! Allah upon him, he is no sultan, but a puppet of the French, a tool in the hands of those who surround him! It is the French Resident-General who rules Maroc!"

"And a very fine man he is, Hajj Muhammad," said Solomon.

"He is a good man, for I have talked with him," said the saint, more quietly. "But he does not know what is going on under the surface, and is helpless. Now, swear to us that you, and these friends of yours, will keep secret what passes here."

THE INTERPRETER swore us by all sorts of Koranic oaths, and then the holy man plunged into the business of his visit—explaining some of the reasons why these six Arabs were fugitives.

It was an involved affair in each case, naturally. The gist of it all was that a group of three or four men around the sultan influenced him against them, goaded them into action, brought false charges against them, or stirred them up by *agents provocateurs*. What had happened to them, had happened to a dozen more, who were scattered over the country—all of them great men. Wealth seized, lands confiscated, crimes committed—an incredible tale, but true. The pashas, or chief judges, were appointed by the sultan, and obeyed his will blindly.

"Now," went on Hajj Muhammad, "here is the meat of the nut, sidi. A conspiracy has been formed to overthrow the sultan and to set up in his place another of purer blood, on whom is the blessing of the Prophet—may his name be exalted!"

"Stop," said Solomon placidly. "Who has formed this conspiracy?"

"It is a sworn secret among some half-dozen chiefs from south to north," said the saint. "I know of it; one other of these my friends knows of it—the rest do not. When the time comes, they will be brought into it—until then, it is kept secret."

The six Arabs stirred, shot looks one at another, were obviously uneasy. Solomon chuckled.

"And you are not so sure about it yourself, Hajj Muhammad," he said. The saint scowled at him. "This conspiracy is fomented by one man. Who?"

"That I cannot tell you."

"Then I shall tell you," said Solomon, his blue eyes wide and unblinking. "This man is John Gayland, whom you call El Gezar, the Butcher. He is manager and governor of the lands owned by Captain Maillot, and lives at the castle of Helal. At this place the rifles and munitions are stored."

Hajj Muhammad stared as though petrified. The other Arabs

sat blinking at Solomon in utter amazement. He held a match unconcernedly to his pipe.

"Now, then," he went on, "does Maillot know about all this or not?"

"Allah upon him, he does not!" snapped the saint, rousing himself from his spell. "How do you know these things?"

"By the power of the Seal of Suleiman," and Solomon held out his hand, upon which was the gold ring graven with the interlaced triangles. "I shall tell you more. Through you and your allied chiefs, this El Gezar can cause an uprising of fifty or sixty thousand armed men upon a certain day. He will furnish machine guns and automatic rifles, which are now in Casablanca, and more are on the way. I can go on and tell you further details; of what use are they? What I want to know is this: Is Maillot in this plot?"

"He is not!" cried Hajj Muhammad, who was excited, suspicious, alert. "And I have no liking for the plot, by Allah! Nor have these men my friends."

"Nor," added Solomon, his blue eyes twinkling at Hassan, "has the son of El Biskri—he whom you have chosen to sit upon the throne of Morocco."

Now there was a sudden dread silence, and hands crept under brown jellabs as though seeking hidden weapons, until Solomon waved his pipe in the air and spoke quietly.

"Come! We have sworn an oath; let us talk frankly. You, Hajj Muhammad, are tempted by this plot. So are your friends. And yet you have misgivings; am I not right? You know that you might sweep the French into the sea, as Krim swept the Spaniards, but that more would return. And yet your friends are desperate. Am I right?"

"You are right, Sidi Solomon," said the saint in a low voice.

"Good. Now you have heard that El Gezar expects to find the vast treasures of Mulai Ismail, which he will place in the hands of the new sultan. Is that right?"

Hajj Muhammad blinked, and his jaw dropped in amazement. Solomon chuckled.

"Well, he will not find those treasures. I have found them myself; rather, my friends here have found them. Ali! Call in the scribe."

The red-headed interpreter went out and came back with the secretary. Solomon now told each of the chieftains to dictate his grievances, beginning with young Hassan. Each obeyed, and each affixed his seal to the sheet of paper handed him to read over. Hajj Muhammad had no grievance; he was simply the most holy saint in a country of saints, and more men obeyed him than the sultan. Solomon took the papers and held them up.

"I am here to help you, in the name of Allah," he said quietly, and looked at his watch. "Now tell me; if these wrongs were to be redressed, if those who caused this injustice were to be punished, would you still seek to rebel against the power of France and bring ruin on Maroc?"

One by one the six answered, beginning with Hassan. Their answers were the same, "No!"

"Then," said Solomon, "when you leave here go away quietly, say nothing of what has passed, and hold aloof from this revolt. If you do this, your wrongs will be redressed inside of thirty days."

"What?" exclaimed Hajj Muhammad. "How do we know this?"

"Because I say it," said Solomon. "And in exactly seven minutes I shall give you proof of my ability to keep my word, if I am alive. Ali, a French gentleman is coming here in seven minutes, more or less. Be at the door to admit him properly."

Ali went out. Keyes lighted a cigaret and drew a long breath.

"John, you've got me beat!" he exclaimed in English. "I can see now how the treasure is mixed up in it, and I can understand—"

"You don't understand a thing, sir," cut in John, with a trace of irritation. "Beggin' your pardon, sir, it ain't what it seems—"

and will you 'ave the goodness to speak French or else keep your mouth shut? These 'ere gents are mortal suspicious."

The Arabs were talking excitedly among themselves. Then Hajj Muhammad spoke harshly.

"Sidi Suleiman, how can we tell that you are not a spy of the Resident-General? He is here in Marrakesh, and it may be that when you report to him he will guard the gates and seize these men."

"In the name of Allah, have a care!" said Solomon, and now his voice was suddenly edged with steel. "Have your friends draw the hoods of their jellabs over their faces—quick! This man must not recognize them."

The six men moved their ungainly garments, drawing up the hoods. A moment later the door was thrown open and into the room came a Frenchman all in white from sun-helmet to shoes, a stick in his hand. He was alone; a handsome man, elderly, who glanced around and then strode forward to Solomon, removing his topee and extending his hand.

"This is M. Solomon?" he said, smiling. "I expected to find you alone—no matter. I know Hajj Muhammad, and shall be glad of a word with him also."

"Good lord!" muttered Keyes, and dug his elbow into me. "The Resident-General—alone with this gang! Get your gun ready!"

CHAPTER X

PISTOL POLITICS

I TOLD KEYS to shut up, and he did. Solomon introduced us to the gentleman who governed Morocco, and
who exchanged salutations with Hajj Muhammad. The six Arab
figures drew a keen look from him, but their faces were covered,
and he took the seat which Solomon offered him.

"We may speak freely?" he said, with a glance at me and
Keyes.

"These gentlemen are friends of mine," returned Solomon.
"They are fully informed."

"Very well," said the Resident, accepting a cigarette. I could
see that the saint was absolutely stupefied at this appearance. "I
understand from certain—er—authorities in Paris that you may
be in a position to solve some of our problems of administration
here, *monsieur*. If so, we shall be grateful."

I caught a significant look that he exchanged with Solomon.
The interpreter had moved to the other side of the room and was
sitting beside Hajj Muhammad, informing him of what passed.

"Yes, Your Excellency," returned Solomon. "I hope that you
will see fit to co-operate with me?"

"With all my heart!"

"In that case, I should like a military pass which will give me
permission to circulate freely through any zone. I want the same
pass for five of my friends." Solomon took up a paper from the
table. "Here is the list."

The Resident glanced at it, and his brows lifted as he shot a look at the holy man.

"For Hajj Muhammad as well? But, *m'sieu*, between you and me—"

"I am aware of that, Your Excellency," said Solomon, his face quite blank. The Resident looked at him a moment, then shrugged.

"Oh, very well! You shall receive the passes in the morning. I suppose you have discovered nothing?"

"Everything," said Solomon. "But I must handle it in my own way."

I saw a little stir among the Arabs as these words were translated. The Resident, however, frowned sharply.

"My dear sir," he said, "I think you forget my position. Must I remind you—"

Solomon sighed wheezily. "Your Excellency," he returned, "I think you forget the authority that was given me before I left Paris. I should greatly regret having to make use of it. As to your position, sir, it may not be what you think it is. Do you know that a revolt is imminent over the entire country, that guns and ammunition are ready in plenty, that plans are drawn up in detail, and that you are face to face with an uprising in every city and district in Morocco—and a massacre of Christians!"

"Good God!" exclaimed the Resident, inexpressibly shocked by this blunt speech. "Are you—is this serious, *monsieur?* Would the native dare such a thing?"

At the other side of the room there was immobility, but the cloaked, hawklike features of the Arabs were tense and not relaxed; and their attitudes showed me that weapons were in the hands under their robes, ready for use. Was Solomon betraying them to their very faces!

"No, the Arabs would not dare—but the French would," said Solomon calmly. "Don't you breathe a word of this affair, Your Excellency, or we are all lost! Certain Frenchmen are behind this whole thing. They have imported arms and ammunition. They have drawn up plans. They are making use of certain Arabs. For what reason? To provoke a revolution which must be punished by blood and fire. To throw Morocco from a civil government into the hands of the military arm. Undoubtedly certain native leaders are involved in this scheme, which will allow them to pillage their enemies and increase their wealth; but your own countrymen are behind it."

"*Monsieur*, this is outrageous!" exclaimed the Resident, flushing. "No Frenchman would so demean himself—"

"All men are men, Your Excellency—especially where gold and power is concerned."

The Resident turned and looked at Hajj Muhammad, and spoke in Arabic. The holy man made a curt assent, then went on in a biting, acid voice.

"So!" The Resident looked again at Solomon. "I am to leave this—this incredible situation in your hands?"

"Unless you do, I go back to Paris."

"Very well. What do you wish me to do about it?"

"Nothing about it; but two things to help me, sir." Solomon took up the six signed sheets of paper with their Arabic characters. "I want you to investigate these complaints yourself, not through any commission. The natives have confidence in you; show them that you deserve it, and you win them. In this case let us have justice, not law. Do you understand?"

"Very well." The Frenchman's tone was bitter. "I understand that you are practically giving orders to me, the Resident-General of Morocco—"

Solomon leaned forward and his blue eyes twinkled as he put his hand familiarly on the Frenchman's knee.

"Exactly, *monsieur*," he said. "And I can only do it because you are a great man, above all personal considerations—a true son of France."

The face of the Resident warmed into sudden cordiality, and his hand went out to that of Solomon.

"Very well, *monsieur.* And the second thing you required of me?"

"A personal and private interview with the sultan, one week from today, in Rabat. I may want to bring two friends with me."

The Frenchman whistled softly, then nodded.

"It shall be arranged. And I am to say nothing to the military authorities—"

"Nor to anyone else."

The Resident nodded again and rose. He shook hands all around, gave Hajj Muhammad a word in Arabic, and departed.

I TOOK a cigarette and lighted it, then sat down again. When I looked at Tom Keyes, I felt like laughing; his face was a study. And no wonder. What we had just heard was well-nigh beyond belief. Perhaps we might not have believed it, indeed— except that these other men in the room, so much more vitally concerned, gave it perfect credence. This was obvious in their manner. They did not even ask Solomon about his authority, in fact.

"Sidi!" broke out Hajj Muhammad swiftly. "Is there proof of this thing you have declared before us? What Frenchmen know of our secret?"

"Maillot, for one," said Solomon. The saint shook his long hair and cursed, and the others helped out his vocabulary. "Undoubtedly a number of the military clique are hand in glove with him, and a number of your own pashas."

"And the sultan?" asked young Hassan.

Solomon made a negligent gesture. "No; he is not a fool."

"Then let him remain sultan," said the boy passionately. "I do not want to be a French tool, a mere doll in white garments! By Allah, where is proof of all this?"

"Aye, where is proof?" demanded the fierce Hajj Muhammad.

"You'll get it in time." Solomon drew out the letter and military pass permitting Ahmed ben Zair to circulate freely in the

Souaffine zone. "Here is a letter which my friend took from Maillot's pocket last night. Read it."

He handed it to the interpreter, who gave it to Muhammad. Solomon turned to us and with a chuckle told us what the letter contained, while the Arabs were cursing over it. Ahmed ben Zair was a gentleman here at Marrakesh who kept a native tavern and presumably was a friend of all the radicals and disaffected Arabs; this letter proved that he was a stool pigeon in the French service.

The Arabs exchanged a few words, then rose. They came over and saluted us, smilingly, and then stalked out—all except the saint and young Hassan, who remained. One of them took the letter with him, and Solomon made no objection. He gave the military pass to Hassan.

"You might need this," he said, and Hassan nodded. Meantime the saint remained seated, staring at Solomon. His thin, high-boned face was a mirror of passion and fierce cruelty, and his eyes positively blazed.

"You have saved us from the pit of folly," he observed.

"Dang it!" said Solomon in English. "Werry glad I am as you realize it." Then he looked at us. "I expect as 'ow you gents would like to get shook down, or maybe see the town a bit? You'll find your things in your room, all shipshape—I've give you one together. We ain't got a thing to do till tomorrow, as the old gent said when 'e kissed the pretty 'ousemaid, and maybe not then. So make yourselves to 'ome and show up for dinner at seven."

Keyes and I departed; Solomon made it quite obvious that he wanted a private talk with Hajj Muhammad. The red-headed Ali showed us to a large room fitted in European style, where our things were disposed. Once alone, Keyes gave me a look and a slow smile.

"Hank, I expect you feel about the same way I do?"

"Yeah. Let's us go out down the street, look up a place to have a drink, and find out if it's all real."

"Keno! Lead on, feller."

So we did it, the afternoon being about over anyway. I had spent two days in Marrakesh, so I knew all about the town, and pretty soon we located a French place and looked at each other over a table, and clinked our glasses.

"Real?" I said.

"Real," affirmed Keyes solemnly. And at this instant occurred something as though to impress upon us, in horrible fashion, that very reality which we had doubted.

From somewhere not faraway burst out the frightful and unmistakable scream of a man staring death in the face. It fetched us out of our chairs. A chorus of cries, excited voices, broke upon us; we saw men running, a crowd collecting, not thirty feet distant. We ran to see what was up, shuffling along with the others—the streets of Marrakesh are unpaved sand.

And there we saw a lean, scrawny Arab lying dead. Worse, he had been literally sliced to bits and disemboweled, probably by several knives acting all at once.

"Lord! Let's get back and have another drink," I said in disgust. We shoved out of the throng, and seeing our waiter, asked who had done it. He shrugged.

"Who knows? Some enemy, doubtless. This Ahmed ben Zair was a bad fellow."

I looked at Keyes, he looked at me, and we resumed our seats in silence. Ahmed ben Zair! We knew now why those Arabs had taken the letter and departed so swiftly and smilingly.

"Well, Hank," and Tom fingered his glass musingly, "that chap was the Resident. You realize what it all means—about our little pudgy friend, eh?"

"It means that he's here from Paris on a special job; what is he, then—a private detective or a diplomat?"

"Neither one; a chap with more brains than he seems to have, and a knowledge of Arabs," said Keyes. "But—the colossal nerve of him! Getting the Resident to call upon him and bringing him alone into that room with six men who were ready to kill him—"

"Cut the post mortem," I intervened. "We're in politics now, and no mistake."

"And politics in these parts," said Keyes, "gets taken damned seriously, as witness the gentleman down the street who got carved in segments. So we stick with Solomon?"

"Hell, yes!" I rejoined. "At least, I do. You have somebody else in mind."

He grinned at that.

Where and how Solomon got that house, I never learned for sure. It was a palace, partly furnished in European style, partly in Arab, and it was a gorgeous place on all counts, while the servants provided by Hajj Muhammad left nothing to be desired. The saint was gone when we got back, and seated at the dinner table with Solomon and Jeanne—or rather at the platform, since we ate Arab fashion, with Keyes helping Jeanne— it was difficult to realize that what we had heard and seen was true. Moonfaced, his blank blue eyes devoid of expression, Solomon was cheerful enough, but he was not my notion of a secret service agent.

We reported the demise of Ahmed ben Zair, but Solomon waved it away and refused to talk business until morning. So, after dinner, we got his big Renault out of the garage up the street and all went over to the French town and dropped in at a cinema.

IT WAS late when we returned to the Seven Men, as old Marrakesh is often termed—taking the name from the seven Islamic saints who are buried there. The full moon was high in the sky, and when we had put up the car, Solomon asked Jeanne if she felt like walking. She did, so we all made our way along the sand-streets to the great square before the El Fna mosque—a tremendous place, which by daylight was thronged with caravans and mules and traders, and was now empty and desolate.

We waited at one side, and presently saw Arabs coming into the square by ones and twos, and the moonlight glinted on rifle barrels.

"What's up?" I asked. Solomon chuckled wheezily.

"A werry old ceremony, sir—all the night patrols gather 'ere at midnight and give a signal to shut the city gates and the gates of the quarters."

The patrols met before the mosque, and a voice shouted out something which Solomon translated as: "For Allah and the Seven Men!" Then, with a rippling crash, there was a volley of shots fired in the air, and we heard answering shots from the distant gates of the city, and it was over—a barbaric little ceremony, but impressive. And that ended our first day in Marrakesh.

In the morning we had a conference with Solomon—this amazing man who had apparently been given authority by the French government which outweighed that of the very ruler of Morocco. He made the situation clear enough, now that his mask was off before us. Jeanne had been acquainted with everything; she sat saying little, her eyes upon Solomon with a fascinated air, for she, too, found it difficult to credit the man's astounding position here.

Solomon slurred over his own position very briefly; he was here, he said, to take care of a threatening situation, and until he got into it had not dreamed it was so far developed. Thanks to yesterday's interview, the most influential native chiefs would now hold aloof from any plot, at least for the present; and Hajj Muhammad, the saint whose holiness gave him more power than anyone else in Morocco, was standing pat. Once convinced that Solomon told the truth, that the conspiracy was being fomented not to win freedom but to serve the private ends of Maillot and the rascally little group around the sultan, the saint would then exert his whole weight into the scales on the side of the French.

But, as Solomon pointed out, the position was highly precarious. An untoward incident would set a spark to the powder, and the explosion would be past any control.

"Well," said Keyes. "isn't the remedy simple? Put your information before the government, let them seize the arms and munitions—"

"And 'ave Maillot and 'is bloody friends slip out? Not much," said Solomon drily. "We ain't got to that stage yet. What's more, that wouldn't do no good. These 'ere Arabs are out for blood. If the French step in, they'll pay dear. It's better to let some o' them Arabs do the blood-letting, so to speak, and take the risks. But let's 'ave the thing clearcut, now. It don't do no 'arm to 'ave an understanding, as the old gent said when 'e kissed the butler's wife."

Good enough, Maillot and two or three others, probably the Grand Vizier among them, were at Rabat, apparently innocent of any complicity. At Helal, the old castle which dominated the great estates now in Maillot's ownership, up north in the Atlas between Marrakesh and Meknez, was the actual head of the plot—the man Gayland, or El Gezar.

Solomon painted this gentleman in an unfavorable light. He was an Englishman who had got into some trouble in Egypt and had chucked everything, including his religion. As a renegade, he had helped drill the troops of Abd el Krim, and some said it was thanks to him that Novarro's Spaniards had been driven into the sea, leaving 40,000 men behind them. He had slipped clear of Krim's debacle, and Solomon averred that he had betrayed Krim to the French and thus won a pardon. At all events, he was in command of Helal and its district, with the rank of caid. And he was a nut that would take some cracking. Solomon said that within three days El Gezar could assemble twenty thousand men.

"First off, we ain't got no proof against 'im, except them 'ere arms and munitions," went on Solomon. "And if it comes down to legal measures, we must 'ave proof. We don't want no legal measures, not wi' The Butcher! We want to smash 'im—smash the 'ole ruddy gang with 'im, too. But before doin' that, we want to get some cumulative evidence as to what 'e's doing up there. And we 'ave to move fast. In another day or two, Maillot will know a lot about me—remember, 'e 'as no end o' spies."

"What about Ishmael's treasure?" asked Jeanne.

"I'm a-coming to that, miss," said Solomon. "Werry sorry I am to say it, but I ain't as young as I was. I'd like werry much to go up to Helal meself, but it's a mortal 'ard trip by foot or 'orse or mule—"

Solomon proposed that Tom Keyes should go to Helal with Hassan for guide, posing as a tourist, but first picking up as much information as possible at Casablanca in regard to the Societé Agricole and what might be lying inside its warehouses. For me he had another and very different errand, which hinged upon my recent adventure with Maillot.

The treasure of Ishmael was inextricably bound up with the whole matter, it seemed. With it in their hands, Maillot and El Gezar would have something that appealed to all Moroccans; Maillot hardly wanted it for his own sake, Solomon thought, but he made it clear to us that to the Arab mind the importance of this treasure would be far greater than its intrinsic value. It was a symbol, a link from the past greatness of Morocco. I gathered from all this that Solomon was himself somewhat at sea about the whole business—and he was.

As he said, two wagon-loads of gold would not contain a very great amount of treasure, and it would be devilish hard to dispose of in any underhand way, probably being ancient coins of French or English mintage. If we were to try to locate it and dig it up, we would encounter all sorts of difficulties with the authorities, both French and Sharifian. But Maillot would have none of these difficulties.

"Let 'im get it," said Solomon, his blue eyes steadily upon me. He had not shaved for two days, and his round features were a stubble of white beard. "Play in with 'im, sir—"

"You mean—you really mean to let him get it?" asked Jeanne uneasily.

"Yes, miss, just like that," and Solomon chuckled. "Let 'im play with it, so to speak—and we can take it away from 'im if we want to. Mr. Smith, 'e ain't no fool. I expect you can wangle it, sir?"

"Rather," I said. Solomon held out his hand with the gold ring on it.

"And if so be as you find someone a-wearing this 'ere ring, sir, you can trust 'im."

"But what am I going to do meantime?" asked Jeanne. Solomon patted her bandaged arms.

"You're a-goin' to set 'ere and keep 'ouse, miss," he said.

And with this, she had to be content. That suited me—I wanted no pretty girl mixed up in what promised to be a bloody business before it was ended!

Solomon folded his wrinkled hands over his knee and grew silent. Jeanne looked as though she was a little hurt at Solomon's seeming slight of her importance. I was glad that he had figured out things that way.

CHAPTER XI

OUT OF MARRAKESH

THREE DAYS later—it was early on a Sunday morning—Tom Keyes and I parted company with John Solomon. Our parting took place in front of the great minaret of the Koutoubia, before a crowd of Arabs, and was highly spectacular.

The three of us had walked over to the generous square tower, and I left them for a closer look at the entrance. The noise of a furious altercation drew me, and I saw Solomon and Keyes with a curious crowd looking on; both of them had lost their heads. I attempted to intervene, and Solomon in a rage, turned on me and gave me a crack in the face that sent me sprawling. When I got to my feet, two Arab policemen were ordering hostilities to cease, while Solomon was cursing me and Tom in French.

"March!" he shouted at us, shaking his fist frantically. "Out of my house, you worthless rogues—out of my house this moment! Get your things and depart!"

"Gladly, *m'sieu*," I said with dignity, wiping the blood from my cut mouth. "You are an old fool of an Englishman, and I leave you with pleasure. Adieu!"

Keyes and I stalked back to the Dar ben Daoud, got our things, and went on to the Transat hotel, where I telephoned for a car.

"Not so bad," observed Keyes. "I saw Jeanne for a minute—a big box of flowers had just come with Maillot's card. So he knows where we are, and about her accident."

"Maillot isn't here in Marrakesh?" I answered. He shrugged.

"Hardly; he'd have been around in person. Probably telephoned an order."

Our ordered car arrived; we threw in our bags, and in five minutes were heading north out of Marrakesh.

We took with us a very definite warning. This business of ours demanded not only diplomacy and caution, but also prompt action at need. If anything went wrong, we could expect no help. We were working for Solomon, and neither he nor we were French government agents—in case of trouble. For the moment all was well. No search was being made for Keyes, and I was confident that our scene with Solomon would be reported to the right quarter.

At Casablanca we parted. I hired a little Citroen from a dealer Keyes knew, and went on to Rabat, getting there in time for dinner at the Transat. I had a sheaf of passports, government permits, military passes and whatnot—all the papers necessary to satisfy the reddest of red tape anywhere in Morocco. Also, I had Maillot's silenced revolver, and a gun of my own.

From the hotel, I telephoned Maillot's villa and got a lady on the line. She said that Maillot was in Meknez, but was charmingly innocent of where to find him. In fact, she was altogether too dumb, so it was plain that she was suspicious. I promptly gave her my name and asked her to get word to Maillot that I would be at the Transat in Meknez, and wanted very much to see him.

If he were at Meknez, this meant that he was working away on his treasure clue. I chuckled and went on in to dinner, intending to spend the night here, and go on to Meknez in the morning. However, I had barely given my order when in came the hotel manager and shook hands.

"It is a pleasure to see you again, Mr. Smith," he said genially. "You are not, by any chance, bound for Meknez tonight?"

"I'll stay here, if you have room." I said. He shrugged.

"Oh, as to that—I inquired, because there is an Englishman who has just arrived in an old car which has broken down. He is most anxious to reach Meknez tonight, and I suggested to him that you might be going on. Stay—there he is now."

"Bring him over," I said.

The manager complied. The Briton was an enormous chap, even taller than I—he must have been a good six feet three, and beautifully built. He had grayish yellow hair, a big yellow mustache, and a face that had reddened under the sun instead of tanning. He had a big square chin, a distinct whiskey mouth, and very light gray eyes which were anything but pleasant.

"Smith, eh?" he said, as we were introduced. "Brown's my name. Should have a Jones here, what? May I dine with you?"

"Delighted," I said, and he dropped into a chair opposite me. He wore comfortable old tweeds and leather puttees. "You're a tourist?"

"More or less," he said. "Doing the country a bit—I've been up in the hills, and my car went to pieces on me today. Got in too late to find a garage open, and I'm devilish keen on reaching Meknez tonight—want to join a friend of mine there."

"Good enough," I said. "In that case, I'll go on to Meknez and we'll make it together."

I studied Brown during dinner, and decided that it was just as well we were going no farther than Meknez in company. He soaked up cognac like a sponge and talked freely enough about everything except himself; indeed, he seemed glad to be able to talk English, and said that he had been pushing about the interior of the country for some months by himself.

"Isn't it dangerous?" I asked. He stared at me, fingered his mustache, and laughed.

"Not a bit, if you can handle yourself. These native swine have a healthy respect for any man who kicks 'em hard, you know."

THAT WAS his philosophy, and evidently he lived up to it. His hands were large-knuckled and hard, he had a scar or two on his face, and he had an arrogant swing to him generally. He was far from being any Lord Chesterfield, and was rather the Thackeray version of Richard Coeur-de-Lion—a handsome big brute who could and would knock anyone out of his way. I fancied that he might once have been a gentleman in the dim past, but he was not the sort who keeps up a pretense; he had long since relapsed into savagery, and did not even have table manners—he had probably eaten native fashion so long that forks had slipped from his memory.

Still, he was interesting, for he was very forceful and vigorous and displayed an amazing knowledge of the country. Brown was not his name, of course, but he kept off personalities. More than once I fancied a vague dislike as his pale gray eyes swept me; like many Englishmen of his type, he probably cherished a hearty dislike for breezy and informal Americans. I think the truth was that we were like two dogs whose back-hackles rise instinctively at sight of each other.

We finished dinner, had a last drink, and went through into the office to pay for our meal and get off. Several Arabs were loafing about the courtyard fountain inside the gate. One of them stopped Brown, who answered him in Arabic, and I went on. After a moment, Brown joined me at the desk, and chancing to find his gaze on me, I was suddenly startled. In those gray eyes was a pallid flame which told me instantly that something had happened.

A moment after, as I went out to the car, I caught a quickly stifled snatch of talk among the loafing Arabs, and the word "El Gezar." There was my answer—no doubt whatever about it. This Englishman was the renegade of whom we had heard, and he had just been told something about me—probably that I was an enemy of Maillot. For an instant I was alarmed, then I smiled to myself and went on to the car. Fate was playing into my hands, it seemed!

Certainly, I might have guessed from his very looks and manner who this man was; for there was all his history written plain to see. He was a thoroughly bad egg—but he was by no means to be discounted.

His car was near mine at the curb—a battered old flivver,

about the only kind of car which could get in or out of the hills. El Gezar came stalking out and got a bag from his car and threw it into mine, climbed in beside me, and we were off. He was silent for a time, until we were across the bridge and on the Meknez highway. Then he started in to question me, displaying an interest in my doings which he had not previously shown. I thought best to spike his guns at the start.

"I'm trying to locate a chap who's somewhere in Meknez now," I said casually. "A Frenchman named Maillot. I've got some information that will make him sit up, if he and I can come to a bargain. It's something of a personal nature, so I can't go into it. Know him?"

"I've heard of him," said El Gezar cautiously, and lost all interest in me, apparently.

This had settled him for the time, and we were both satisfied. I had no doubt now that I would hear from Maillot in the morning, for of course El Gezar knew where to find his chief. All the way over to Meknez he was extremely careful as to his utterances; evidently he was not too well acquainted with what had been going on lately, and dared take no chances.

When we got to Meknez, following the highway that circled around to the left of the walls and cemetery, El Gezar had me pull up at the Bab el Jedid—the lower gate of the old city, directly opposite the Transat hotel on the hill. Several carriages were in sight, late as the hour was, and El Gezar transferred his bag to one of these—he was going somewhere in the medina, though he did not say where. We shook hands, he thanked me for the lift, and I went on to the Transat, where a room had been reserved for me by telephone.

I was dog tired after my long day, and tumbled into bed at once. I could not get to sleep for some time, however; and even after I was asleep, the figure of El Gezar went stalking through my dreams. This man might not be as powerful as the crafty and suave Maillot, but he was a remarkably dangerous person. His massive reddened features, his terrible pale eyes, lingered with me. His Arab name of "the butcher" was probably well deserved. Such a man might well plan a country-wide massacre and revolt; your renegade who has turned his back upon his own race and creed is always the most cruel and ruthless of men, with a vicious hatred against those who bred him.

My breakfast came in at eight in the morning, and after I was dressed I took a brisk walk over to the French town—for I was determined not to be hanging around waiting for the pot to boil. There I got a few things I needed, loafed around over an aperitif, and headed back for the hotel. I got there about eleven-thirty, and found Maillot and El Gezar sitting at one of the yellow umbrella-shaded tables on the terrace before the entrance. The fish was hooked.

Maillot got up and came toward me cordially; he had lost any traces of our encounter, and looked very fresh and handsome. Nor, apparently, did he bear any resentment—though I knew well enough there was hatred in his heart.

"Come, welcome to Meknez!" he exclaimed, shaking hands heartily and giving me an amused look. "Singular that we should be on a friendly footing after recent events, eh? But nonsense; we're men and not children. Will you join us?"

"Gladly," I said. Maillot took my arm familiarly, and lowered his voice.

"It's all right, Smith," he said. "I know what happened in Marrakesh yesterday morning, so no explanations. You know M. Brown, I think? El Gezar, as the Arabs call him—he rather prefers the nickname. Natives are given to that sort of thing, you know."

Brown showed yellow fangs under his yellow mustache and shook hands, and I sat down. This was the safest place to talk, the tables being well out in front of the hotel, on the terrace sloping down to the road. When I had ordered a drink and the Arab waiter was gone, Maillot held a match for my cigarette.

"Such is life in Morocco!" he exclaimed whimsically. "El

Gezar, a few days ago we were at each other's throats; today we talk amicably. So you came to seek me, M. Smith?"

"Yes," I said, and hesitated. Maillot laughed.

"Oh, don't hesitate to speak! El Gezar is the manager of my farms—a sort of junior partner, as it were. He's fully acquainted with everything, and if you like, we can lay our cards on the table. Eh?"

I nodded. Maillot was laying down no cards, but it was my place to let his imitation frankness take me in completely, and I flatter myself that I did a good job of it. He was infernally curious to find out why I was here. I think he was on edge to know all he could learn about Solomon's activities.

"Well," I said, to feel him out, "of course you're aware what Solomon is doing in Maroc."

He shrugged. "The fat little Englishman? I know little about him. You and your friend Keyes, however, have made a good deal of trouble."

"I've come out of it with some real information, all the same," I responded. "That is, if you're interested in buried treasure."

"Ah! Who is not?" Maillot exchanged a flashing glance with El Gezar. "Come, my friend! Why not be frank about it? You know well enough where my interest lies."

"Exactly," I returned. "Solomon thinks he's on the verge of finding out about that treasure of Ishmael; meantime, I have found out."

"What?" Maillot gave me a sharp look. "You know where it is?"

"Absolutely. You procured a certain document—but part of it had been cut off as being worthless. I found it and destroyed it, after getting it translated. Now we can talk business, perhaps."

Maillot's eyes glistened, but he made a gesture of caution. The waiter was coming.

"Undoubtedly. Just what is the Englishman doing in Morocco?"

"Oh, he came here for his health," I responded, as our drinks were sat down. "Then the young lady, who knew him, called him into the matter, and now he's trying to pull wires and obtain the necessary authorization and so forth—he thinks he knows where to look," and I laughed.

"I understand," said Maillot carefully, "that he is active among the natives."

"He had letters to a number of them, from Arabs in Algiers and elsewhere," I said carelessly covering up the political end of things as far as possible. "He thinks they may help him in finding what we're after. Well he's far wrong there!"

"He certainly is," asserted Maillot, and our glasses were raised. "Health!"

Alone once more, we settled down to business.

"Now, just what do you know?" demanded Maillot.

"Enough," I assured him, "to walk directly to the hiding-place of the treasure—two wagonloads of gold coin."

"Yea?" He chuckled. "Perhaps hidden in the palace walls, eh?"

The tinge of bitterness in his voice told me that I held trumps. He had been deceived by Solomon's little trick and had summoned El Gezar to Meknez; only to find, meantime, there was no treasure at the appointed spot.

"Not at all," I returned coolly. "That wooden box held nothing of value to us, or perhaps the treasure was moved afterward. You forgot the document with Ishmael's seal, Maillot. What seemed to be a riddle, was actual fact. I can read that riddle, if it's worth your while."

The pale gray eyes of El Gezar were watching me closely. Maillot's face lighted up eagerly, and he leaned forward.

"Yes? And the answer to it—"

I LEANED back in my chair and laughed softly.

"Come, come! You're not dealing with a child, Maillot. We're talking business, not philanthropy. What's it worth to you?"

"A percentage?" he demanded.

"Not much," I said. "What would I do with a lot of gold

coin? I'm talking Bank of France notes. In return, I can take you directly to where the gold is hidden—if it's still there."

Maillot glanced at his lieutenant, and El Gezar nodded.

"Go ahead. He's telling the truth."

"I am," was my response. "Of course, I can't guarantee that the gold hasn't been found since it was hidden. What about the practical end of the job? You have authority to search? And if you find it, what about—"

Maillot waved his hand impatiently.

"Never mind; I have full authority, in a special permission from the sultan," he said. "I find it better to do any searching at night, because there are always curious natives around, and we don't want to get the reputation of treasure-hunters. Well, you will undertake to find the spot, eh? At what price?"

"What's it worth to you?" I asked cautiously.

"Ten thousand francs."

I put down my glass, shoved my chair back, and stared at him.

"What? Listen, my friend, are you looking for a batch of old copper money, or for two wagonloads of gold? I'm not talking business with anyone—"

"Well, well, name your price!" snapped Maillot, his eyes flashing.

"Fifty thousand francs, cash."

"Hm!" He eyed me, startled by such a sum. "Before or after?"

"After it's located; before you move it."

He drummed on the table with his fingers for a moment, then nodded quickly.

"Done. My car is here; suppose we run over now and look at the ground. Then we can come back here for luncheon, and I'll make arrangements for workmen and so on, this afternoon. Tonight we can attack the job. Eh?"

I nodded.

We passed through the hotel to the circular drive behind, where our cars were located, and all three of us got into Mail-

lot's Citroen. As we headed for the old city, he asked where we were going.

"I don't know yet," I said, with a laugh. "Haven't been to see. Do you know of any sun dial in or about the palace grounds?"

El Gezar uttered a grunt.

"There's what used to be a sun dial behind the stables," he said, "in front of the reservoir. Nothing is left of it except the brass plate, and part of that has been torn away. Is that the place?"

"Let's go and see," I returned.

We cut through the medina and turned into the palace grounds at the Filala gate, passing the green-tiled tomb of old Ishmael. We went on between the enormous walls he had built, with those of the seraglio on one hand, those of the palace gardens on the other, the road a narrow lane between, and so came to what El Gezar, in common with most guides, called the stables of Ishmael. In reality this gigantic structure, now roofless but with its hundreds of great pillars and arches still standing, had been an enormous granary; the ruins of his stables, which had held 12,000 horses, were some distance off.

Here we left the car and made our way around the tremendous walls of the granary to the desolate and empty space behind it. To our left was the alleged reservoir—in reality an artificial lake constructed by Ishmael and surrounded by elaborate gardens—probably patterned on those of Versailles, which his various embassies to Louis XIV had vastly admired. Now every-thing was in ruins or vanished—a few clumps of stone here and there in a deserted field alone bearing witness of what had been the gorgeous pleasure-ground behind the palace.

El Gezar knew his way, however, and led us to a clump of rocks nearly opposite the center of the reservoir. Climbing among these, he brought us to a flat bit of broken masonry, with masses of the ever-present Moroccan cactus about it, and pointed to a broken plate of corroded brass set with large rivets in the cement.

"That shows nothing now," he said, "but I remember seeing it years ago and cleaning it off, and finding the marks of a sun-dial. It had part of an inscription in French."

Both he and Maillot were watching me eagerly. I looked around, and nodded. This was the place, no doubt of it—under our feet was the treasure of Ishmael! Or was it?

CHAPTER XII

BURIED TREASURE

"ALL RIGHT, Maillot," I said. "Here's the place. These rocks once formed part of a grotto, or cave—an artificial one, built here in the gardens. Probably it's all been filled up long ago. The treasure was hidden under this sun-dial, in or about that grotto. That should be exact enough to work upon."

"Good," said the Frenchman, his eyes glinting. "Yes, why not? This was part of the old palace enclosure—all of this space for miles around was within the palace. Ishmael had his wild animal pits close by here, too; easy enough for him to hide that amount of treasure without all the world knowing it! Very well—tonight we shall know for certain."

We made our way back to the car, and retraced our way through the native town again and so to the hotel on the opposite slope. El Gezar soaked up a few cognacs, and we got a table by the windows overlooking Meknez, and so settled down to a more or less triumphant luncheon. There was no discussion of the treasure, naturally—but there was other talk.

Now, my instructions from Solomon were highly elastic. He had practically thrown his orphan boy—Henry Smith—out upon the world to follow his nose, sink or swim, do as he liked and use his brains. I had no reports to make, and had not a ghost of an idea how to make any. It was a rather insane affair to all appearance, but I had an idea that through his Arab friends John Solomon would get all the reports necessary.

And I was beginning to have a good time. Maillot's friendship did not fool me for a minute; just at present I was being useful to him, but sooner or later he would even up the score and pay me what he owed me. I did not mind having him for a secret enemy, nor did I mind having Gayland-Brown-El Gezar in the opposing camp. The Butcher and I simply did not mesh gears to any extent. I could feel that he quite despised me and saw nothing menacing in my long and lanky figure; while the more I saw of him, the more he impressed me with a sharp and active dislike. That long yellow mustache of his, which made him look like a stalwart viking was a constant temptation. Every time I lit a cigarette, I wanted to light that mustache instead.

Before we settled down to luncheon I ran up to my room and got a heavy package wrapped in newspaper, and when our waiter had departed with the orders and the Arab bus-boy had located the hors-d'oeuvres within our reach, I laid this package in Maillot's lap.

"A restitution of stolen property," I said cheerfully, "just to signify that the war is over—that is, if it is!"

Maillot glanced at the silenced revolver, broke into a hearty laugh, and lifted his glass.

"It is over, mon ami!" he exclaimed, but he spoke the last two words in a tone of voice that I recognized. A Frenchman always says "my friend" in that tone to a man whom he is anxious to murder. El Gezar caught it, also, and repressed a smile.

Maillot went on to chatter about one thing and another, was much interested in journalism, and did not hesitate to get me talking about my past life. When El Gezar chipped in with a question about military experience, I saw a great light—his voice was just a little too casual.

Being in Morocco, I did as the Moroccans did; that is to say, I took a leaf from the book of the Transat guides, and I did my best to satisfy curiosity without the least regard for the truth. I never did care particularly about consequences, and in this case it looked as though they would be highly satisfactory; and I was right.

"These Arabs," said Maillot, "are remarkable fighters; and as they showed the Spaniards, they can do wonders if they have the proper direction. El Gezar, there, was all through the Riff business—he knows."

El Gezar grinned, and sounded me out as to how I felt toward the French, and whether I had sympathy for downtrodden natives, and so forth. I gave him the proper replies, without letting on that I had any knowledge under the surface, and I saw him exchange another look with Maillot, this time of satisfaction. The conversation was dropped there, however—Maillot did not want me to suspect that he was connected with any revolutionary ideas.

Luncheon over, the two of them departed about their business, promising to meet me here at six; we would have dinner before taking up the evening's work of treasure hunting. Unless I was far wrong, the two of them were properly impressed with my lack of discretion and my entire willingness to do anything that would give me a line on a big news story—Maillot was a sharp one there. I went to my room and slept away most of the afternoon, and felt pretty proud of Henry Smith's diplomacy.

It was closer to seven than to six when Maillot turned up, alone. He looked serious, and took me into one corner of the big writing-room for a confidential chat. He played his part excellently, I must say.

"I am about to propose something to you, my friend," he said. "It is about this Englishman whom we call El Gezar. You comprehend, he is a good man in many ways, manages my farms and my castle well, and so forth—but rumors have reached me. Helal is off in the Atlas, out of the world, and I cannot afford to have my manager indulging in politics, or making friends with disaffected Arabs. I have heard rumors of native movements up there, and it makes me a trifle uneasy. I do not trust this manager of mine too far, when it comes to politics."

"Yes?" I said encouragingly.

"I wonder whether you would consider going back to Helal with him," said Maillot. "I could send an Arab, but one can never be sure about a native—and if you would visit Helal for a few days, watch El Gezar, stay as long as you like, in fact. I should be very glad to find out whether he is working for me, or working for his own influence among these Berbers. The hill folk are like children, you know, and this man is mad enough to fly off at any tangent."

I reflected solemnly. All this was so well done that, unless I had known what was actually going on beneath the surface, it would have fooled me completely. So I replied that a visit to a castle in the Atlas would be very agreeable, and that I should be most happy to help Maillot if it could be done. This arranged, Maillot spoke of the night's work, said that he could not dine with us as he had an engagement in town, and asked me to bring El Gezar over to the old palace grounds at nine, in my car.

"I have seven trusty men ready," he said, "and they can work excellently by moonlight. If we find anything, I have all arrangements made for more men and a camion, and we can then get the task completed before morning. No one will interfere with us. And now—you will excuse me if I run? We'll meet tonight."

I EXCUSED him, and off he went, and five minutes later El Gezar came up from the carriage entrance. He joined me in the lounge and we ordered a drink to get up our appetites. The big brute had donned a clean shirt and looked quite decent.

"I suppose," he said with clumsy attempts at craft, "that you would not be interested in seeing any of the disaffected natives and hearing their stories?"

"I'd like nothing better," I said eagerly.

"Well, if you'd care to run up to Helal with me, you might do just that, Smith. Quite a few chiefs hang out up there in the hills, you know—chaps who don't love the French. I've heard that a rebellion might break out, but of course that's all tosh. Would it interest you? If so, I'd be glad to have you. But don't say a word to Maillot, mind—that chap is in thick with the sultan and his crowd. He doesn't know half what goes on upcountry; some day he'll wake up with a bang!"

It was plausibly done, and I felt a little cold chill creep up my spine as we talked. It was a revelation of the man facing me—a revelation of his cold-blooded deviltry. For, from those pale gray eyes of his, as though from the pages of a book, I suddenly read the whole thing.

Yes, these things do happen, as every man knows, whether he will admit it or not. Thoughts do jump across empty air—or follow air channels, if you want to put it that way. And in this moment as I sat there, the entire game of these two men leaped out, clearcut and distinct in my mind, as though this brute had told it to me. Perhaps he had told it to me in his very eyes—he was not the kind to shield his clumsy thoughts. Maillot could do that, but not this animal.

I sparred for time, led him into further talk, carried him on in to dinner without making any decision. To tell the truth, I was frightened.

And why not? Maillot was cleverly keeping out of it, as he thought, craftily following his plan of covering his own steps every foot of the way; as Solomon said, he and those who were in the game with him, would always slide out. El Gezar was to take me to Helal, convinced that I would plunge hotfoot into the Arab revolt, for the sake of the excitement and the news story that was in it. Henry Smith and fifty thousand francs up at Helal when the massacre broke—and who would send out the news story? Who would publish to the world that an American adventurer was training the rebels, was with them, leading them? El Gezar would slide out of all this, too. The French would never get his head. The goat in the whole affair, the one to be brought in like a dead wolf, past talking, would be the American—yes, when the time came to exact payment for the country-wide massacre and fighting and murdering, Henry Smith would pay.

I had this vision as we sat there at dinner with the Frenchmen serving us, with tourists babbling at the tables around, with the lights of Meknez gleaming across the valley depths, with the calls of the muezzins lifting and falling from the minarets on the opposite hill. And, smiling into those pale gray, murderous eyes of The Butcher, I suddenly realized for the first time what this reverse of the medal was like.

Behind me stood nothing but Henry Smith—the pudgy little figure of Solomon did not count. I had been warned, of course, but reality is seldom comprehended until we come face to face with it. I was alone. El Gezar, at Helal, was not only powerful; his word was law. Under Maillot's thumb, at his call, was the whole force of the Shariffian state. Keyes might be there at Helal, yes, but—

"Tell you what, Brown—or El Gezar, if I'm to call you that— I'll think this thing over," I said. "It's a temptation, yes; but I'm an impulsive beggar, and if I get to running around with these native rebels or whatever they are, I might jump in and lend 'em a hand," and I laughed, pretending not to see the flash in the brute's eye. "You see, that's the Irish of it, and I've got to keep the Irish down."

"What? Irish?" He frowned at me. He was the type who cannot understand anything but a direct hit. "I thought you were a bally American, old chap—the name Smith and all that—"

"I'll tell you a secret," I said. "Smith isn't my name, or wasn't. You see, I changed my name in youth. My father was a wild Irishman, always fighting around with helpless peoples, always leading an army somewhere against oppression, fighting for freedom as it were—you know, the freedom to fight they never had in Ireland—"

He nodded as I paused to gulp at my wine. "Yes? And his name?"

"I'm coming to that," I said. "You see, his name was too well known. I found that I could never go anywhere without getting pointed out; it clung to me all over the world, and it exerted a sort of hypnotic effect on me. Under the spell of that name I found myself always doing damn fool romantic things, women always making love to me, and so on. The only way out of it I could see was to change my name. So I did. I became plain Smith."

"Yes?" he said, pulling at his long yellow mustache. "And what was your father's name, then? I might know it."

"You might, Brown, you might." I said solemnly. "His name was Jones."

"Eh, what?" He blinked at me. "But, I say! That isn't an Irish name, you know!"

I had wasted a good five minutes on that poor fish. He never did know I was joking.

However, I effected one thing; a gain of time. He came back to the attack once or twice, but I managed to stave him off. For some reason—perhaps premonition—those terrible pale eyes of his, and the thought of going to Helal with him, gave me a shiver. And the more I evaded, the more clearly did I see that he was set on my going to Helal.

Dinner over, we had our coffee in the salon, and then, after a liqueur, went out to my car, and were on our way.

FIFTEEN MINUTES later, we were scrambling over debris behind the granary of Ishmael. With us were Maillot and half a dozen vague and ragged figures—Arabs. The moon, full and glorious, was just rising above the enormous crenelated walls that hemmed us in. One Arab had been left on guard by the car, to keep any curious folk away.

With the light of an electric torch to help start the work, our men fell to the task with pick and shovel. But, to tell the truth, I could not take any too great interest in the present business; at the back of my mind lingered and grew the unpleasant certainty that Maillot was an infernally shrewd devil, and that if I walked into his web at Helal, I was fated to have a bad time. I had heard about these upcountry Arabs, who retained the little manner-isms of their ancestors—the punishment of salt, impalement, blinding with hot iron, and so forth.

And, unless I missed my guess, this renegade El Gezar was not the man to call a halt on such things.

No, I would be a fool to put my head into the noose, and I definitely made up my mind there in the moonlight, amid the ruins of Ishmael's gardens, that I would not fall into the trap. After this decision, which I kept to myself, I felt better.

The hollow clang of picks on stone re-echoed through the moonlight; the great sheet of water, where once the pleasure-barges of Ishmael had moved, glittered peacefully, and owls hooted from the cavernous depths of the gigantic granary. After an hour of labor, the mass of rocks showed little evidence of what had been done. The platform of masonry was destroyed and ripped aside, the few feet of soil below was cleaned out, and we were down to a huge mass of large rocks, apparently piled there loosely and cemented together. Maillot was obviously perturbed by this discovery.

"It looks like a *poisson d'Avril*," he said gloomily to me, as we watched the uncovering of that rocky mass.

"An April fool joke? Nonsense!" I returned cheerfully. "Just the contrary, Maillot! Old Ishmael was not the man to dump his treasure into a hole in the ground and leave it for anyone to scratch up. Those rocks are not natural and they're not naturally placed. Rocks of such large size don't cement themselves together. Now, depend on it, we'll find that they've been built up in this fashion to conceal the grotto mentioned."

"Perhaps," he said. "But breaking into them is a slow process. If there was a grotto, it must have had an entrance."

"And in the course of two hundred years," I retorted, "all this expanse of gardens has been destroyed and filled up, buried under debris. We don't know where the entrance was—all we can do is to smash a way down through the top."

He nodded. "Oh, of course! And one thing is absolutely certain, my friend—nobody has been here ahead of us!"

No mistake about that, either. The work now became laborious in the extreme, and could not be done rapidly. Two of the men had to go back to the medina for more tools—hammers and wedges. Each of the enormous masses of stone had first to be knocked clear of its setting, and then had to be worked aside out of the way. This done, the setting itself had to be cleared, and here came encouraging evidence.

The mortar employed was not the usual mastic, as it was termed, of Ishmael's general construction—earth and sand mixed with lime and pounded down wet into a mass, which degenerates with time and softens up. This mixture was hard as rock, and was obviously composed of sand and gravel mixed with a true cement, such as would have been used by a Christian slave anxious to make a good job of it.

It was getting on to two o'clock when our men got down to another mass of the same big rocks. By this time it was perfectly clear that there was no earthly chance of getting through before daylight, and El Gezar, with a yawn, swaggered over to where Maillot and I stood.

"This is all folly," he declared. "Let me come over here tomorrow with a charge of gelatinite. I'll run a wire to the road and explode it from there, and clear out. It won't make too much of a racket, and nobody will know where it has come from; post a guard or two, if you want to make sure. Then we can come with a dozen men after dark, and clear out the stuff. We'll either be down to the treasure, or we'll find there isn't any."

Maillot weighed this advice, asked my opinion, and I backed up the renegade. So it was decided: and calling off our men, we knocked off work for the night.

I saw nothing of either Maillot or El Gezar the next day until, late in the afternoon, Maillot telephoned to ask if I would come for dinner with them, at the house of a native. I accepted promptly, for there is nothing better than good Arab cooking. About dark I got in the car, drove over to the medina, and picked up El Gezar outside the marvelous El Mansur gate—that restored entrance to Ishmael's palaces which still bears the name of the Christian renegade who built it. He grinned as he climbed in beside me.

"I blew bally hell out of those rocks," he said. "Didn't make too much of a noise, either. If all goes well, I'll be on my way to Helal with a camion of gold by morning. Better make up your mind to run up there with me. Smith."

"I've made up my mind not to go," I said. "Do you aim to take the gold upcountry?"

"Yes—we don't want the sultan to grab it, and he's getting a split of the treasure already, bad luck to him!" growled the big brute. "We want to use the gold for prestige—no end of moral influence, you know, in having Ishmael's treasure on display. All the chiefs would sell their shirts for a part of it."

So—he meant to pay off some of the rebel chiefs with Ishmael's money! His words and actions very clearly revealed just what were his intentions, and just what he would do if we found some of the buried gold of Ishmael. El Gezar had a plan alright.

WE HAD not far to go, and were received by a stately old Arab or Berber, with grizzled red hair and bright blue eyes, who brought us through his house to the bedroom-dining-room where we found Maillot waiting. There were no other guests. Slaves waited on us, the sons of the house stood around watching, and we enjoyed a bangup dinner. As our host spoke no French, I did not have much share in the conversation, but I gathered that El Gezar was really the guest of honor. Because of his former position with Abd el Krim and his part in that gentleman's victories he was something of a hero all over Morocco.

I was an expert at dismembering chickens and scooping up artichoke leaves with my right hand only, although I could not knead the *couscousu* into a ball, balance it, and jerk it up to my mouth as the others could. The meal ran its course, we adjourned to a salon for mint tea, and then Maillot got us off, for it was nine o'clock, and he was impatient.

The three of us drove under Ishmael's walls to our destination, and there by the roadside found a dozen Arab workmen wait-

ing, with their tools. We headed them across the open ground
and came to our goal—and perceived that El Gezar's charge
had certainly accomplished its purpose. The mass of rocks had
been split and smashed, and were half buried in debris, which
the workmen attacked at once.

I was standing a little apart, looking on, and was lighting a
cigarette when one of the Arabs dropped his pick and came
quickly to me, jerking a cigarette butt from behind his ear and
asking for a light. I gave it to him, and felt him slip a folded
paper into my hand. He grinned and held before my eyes a
golden circlet—the ring of Solomon. Then he was gone, back
to work.

I had no means of reading the note, if such it were; the moonlight was brilliant, but more than moonlight was needed—I had
to have privacy as well. So, putting it away, I gave my attention to
the work; and soon had enough to keep me occupied. The Arabs
were making rapid progress with their clearance—and suddenly
one of them uttered a shout, half of fear, half of exultation, as he
sank clear to his shoulders and then came scrambling out again.
They were through the shell of cemented rocks.

Now excitement rose high, and the Arabs pitched in like good
fellows. Inside of another half hour there was a hole cleared in
the rubble a good yard wide, and taking the electric torch, I
went to the edge, with Maillot and El Gezar beside me. Peering
down, we made out what must have been a small cave or grotto;
the floor of it, however, was only two feet under the upper shell.
Then El Gezar uttered an exclamation.

"I say, look there! It's no floor, after all! Put down the light,
Smith—"

I leaned over and held the torch down. Then we all saw
plainly—what seemed to be the floor was in reality the top of
chests, placed side by side; we counted them in growing excitement, and there must have been a dozen small ones, with one
very large iron or brass chest at the end.

"Good," said Maillot, straightening up. "We've found the

treasure. Here, El Gezar—we'd better send off and have that camion brought up at once. It will take some time to increase the size of this hole and—"

Here was my chance, as they moved back. I got out the note and opened it, holding it down so that the curious Arabs could not see what I was doing. It was a scrawl in French:

"M. Keyes killed last night in Rabat. Return Marrakesh."

Keyes—killed!

I straightened up and looked around. Maillot and El Gezar were talking at one side, the Arabs were pressing forward to peer into the hole. I quickly identified the man who had shown me the ring, for he wore a white *jellab* while the others wore dark weaves or burlap. I caught his arm and pulled him aside.

"You have the ring?" I asked, to make sure. He fished it out of his mouth and showed it. "All right. Go back and say that I am going to Helal with El Gezar—and by the lord, I'll make him pay for murdering my friend! That's all."

He nodded and slipped away, and I stood there in the moonlight, repressing the grief and fury that filled my heart. Good old Tom Keyes killed! All right. I would walk into the trap—and Allah help the murderous devils!

CHAPTER XIII

ISHMAEL'S GOLD

THE ARABS fell to work again, attacking the shattered rocks with renewed vim; one of them departed to town in search of the truck. El Gezar came up to me, suppressed excitement in his voice.

"Well, Yank, what about it?" he demanded. "Last chance to change your mind, you know—we'll load up and be off in a hurry. We'll want to get the stuff out of town and into the hills as quickly as possible. Think you'll go along and have a look-see at the Atlas?"

"Yes," I said. "I'll go, and thank you for the chance. What about Maillot?"

"Oh, leave that to me—I'll tell him you're running up to Helal for a day or two to visit me," and the blond brute swung off to direct the excavation.

I joined Maillot. Excited as he was, the Frenchman did not forget his caution where I was concerned. When I said that I was going to take up his proposition and go to Helal, he drew me off to one side, apparently beyond earshot of El Gezar.

"Excellent!" he said warmly. "Now, remember, see everything you can; it's a pity you don't speak Arabic, but that can't be helped. And don't let El Gezar suspect that you're spying on him or on what he does. If you have a camera, take some pictures of any natives who may be swaggering around. I'm really uneasy about the situation there."

"Yet," I said drily, "you're letting this chap take the treasure there?"

"Oh, that's safe enough," he said, disconcerted for a moment but rallying quickly. "You see, I've promised the sultan a personal and private split if we find anything. He won't want any of his councilors to know about it, and we must rush it through to Helal before anyone suspects. Then El Gezar will send down the sultan's third, and so forth. The chap is honest enough as regards money, but I don't trust him with the natives."

It was pretty lame, but was guaranteed to fool an American tourist, as he considered me. In reality, of course, he never intended giving the sultan any split whatever. Either he and El Gezar would salt it all away, pending their rebellion, or else they would use some of it with the disaffected chiefs. However, I professed myself quite satisfied with his explanation, and asked about my fifty thousand francs.

"I have it here," he said, fumbling at his wallet, and produced a fat sheaf of notes. "Here, take it; we've found the gold, and no mistake. Do you want to get your things from the hotel? El Gezar will take the truck from here and start the minute it's ready. You might go with him and pick up his car at Rabat, if it's repaired."

"No, thanks," I said. "I've seen that bus of his. What kind of a truck have you got?"

"A good new Ford truck," he returned. "Why?"

"Then I'll take the truck," I said, "and El Gezar can pick up his own flivver at Rabat. Will you take care of my car? I hired it at Casablanca—"

"I'll have it returned, yes," he promised. "Now, if you want to get your bag, better start after it. El Gezar has his bag in the truck already. We don't want to lose a minute getting the stuff away from here—"

"Aren't you going to look into the chests?"

He laughed. "At my Rabat villa. We'll open one of them there.

I'll leave my car here and drive on there with you, and El Gezar can bring the truck. Eh?"

"Fine," I said, and swung away.

Tom Keyes dead! This recollection damped all my exultation over having found the treasure; nor did it cause me any particular excitement anyway, for it was not my treasure. How it had happened or why, did not matter; now I had an incentive to pit myself against these two rogues, and no mistake, for somebody was going to pay dearly. Tom's death had jerked the whole game into my hands, for Solomon had to sit in Marrakesh, pull the strings, and take care of himself.

"Very good!" I laughed as I swung the car around and headed between the palace walls for the medina. "Get me in a trap, will they? Then somebody will wish to hell they'd never got me into it, before I'm through!"

I made all speed over to the Transat, checked out, threw my bag into the car, and put my pistol in my pocket. Then I was off again, retracing my course—by this time I was getting to know all the ins and outs of Meknez. I went roaring down between the palace walls and found a shiny truck drawn up beyond the towering granary. Two chests were aboard, and others were on the way.

At the excavation everyone was busy getting out the chests. These were, with one exception, all very small, but it took four men to get each one over to the truck. I figured that a large proportion of the weight was in these massive chests, and I was right. The one exception, the large brass or copper chest, was lighter, and much larger. Maillot laughed as he looked at it.

"Who knows?" he said, pointing to it. "That may be one of the coffers which old Ishmael put to a practical use. When he had any trouble with his five hundred wives, he would make them kneel against an open chest with their breasts across the edge, and then would slam down the lid. On at least one historic occasion, the victims were made to eat their own flesh thus cut off. Well, times have changed, happily!"

"What's in that chest?" I asked. Maillot gave me a queer look in the moonlight.

"I have a certain suspicion," he returned. "But it's not one to be settled here, so we'll not look into it now. Here, take a hammer and some of those tools to the truck, and smash open the last of the small chests to go aboard—than we can look into it later. Perhaps on the road will be better than at Rabat; in that way, there'll be no stop in town."

I obeyed him, and El Gezar came to my assistance. The small chests were all loaded aboard the truck, and we tackled the rear-most, as the Arabs made them fast with ropes. We smashed the whole lid in proper fashion, and El Gezar threw it up, to show a glimpse of musty and rotted cloth; then, with a grin, he closed it again and helped arrange a tarpaulin over the whole load, big chest and all.

"You have the papers?" asked Maillot, joining us. "Then go ahead and we'll pick you up at the gate. I'll pay off these men."

El Gezar leaped into his seat, started the engine, and was off with his load of gold.

Five minutes later, we followed him, Maillot sitting beside me, breathing hard with the excitement that had been on him. He would have been still more excited if he knew that among those workmen had been one of John Solomon's spies.

TO TELL the truth, I did not see just what I would be able to accomplish by this trip to Helal, so far as Solomon was concerned, and did not care particularly. I was out now to smash anything I could reach—when the time came. This traitorous Frenchman, who could deliberately plan to let hundreds and thousands of his own people face massacre, and this blond brute of a renegade, would find out soon enough that they had a private war on their hands. My chief task would be, of course, to make Maillot discard his cautious mask—I must draw him into it somehow, use my brains, get him to involve himself!

But of this there was no immediate prospect.

We plunged through the medina and picked up the truck at

the gates, where El Gezar was showing his papers. Maillot was passed, with a salute, and telling El Gezar to follow us, we shot ahead and out on the road for Rabat.

"If I had your chance," I said, as the little Citroen roared along, "I'd ship that stuff aboard a boat and clear out of here. What's to prevent?"

Maillot laughed unpleasantly. "A good deal's to prevent, my friend. The intrinsic value of gold coin is not so great, all things considered; and anyone would have a devil of a time disposing of the gold, remember. Your fifty thousand francs probably represents more than I'll ever see of that treasure in actual cash—but we'll make it earn large dividends. That gold will do us incalculable good, and at a pinch one can always melt it down—"

He cut himself short there and fell silent. Yes, at a pinch it could be melted and turned in to any bank; he was right enough there. But he little guessed that most of the fifty thousand francs were now reposing in the safe of the Transat hotel behind us. That little sum, with what other money I had along, was safely salted away where nobody else could get it.

We were about half way to Rabat when Maillot touched my arm.

"There's a fork in the road ahead," he said. "Turn out, and let the camion come up under our lights; it's good level ground, and we're perfectly safe from interruption at this hour, so we can take a look at what we've found."

I was more than glad of this, and presently the lights of the truck showed up behind us. Maillot, standing out in our headlight glare, waved his arms and El Gezar slowed down and ran in just ahead of our car. It was a lonely countryside spot, no cars were on the road, and we had all the chance we needed.

All three of us attacked the tarpaulin, got it turned back, and went at the chest we had smashed open. El Gezar ripped away the cloth packing, and laid bare a flowing mass of gold coin in the chest. It had been confined in little bags of canvas, but these had long since rotted like the cloth around. I examined some of the coins curiously; all seemed to be sovereigns of Queen Anne's reign.

"Probably the money Ishmael got for slave ransoms," commented Maillot, and stuffed his pockets with the coins. "Some of the other chests will have French and Spanish money—this probably represents what he gleaned during his sixty years' reign. Well, shall we tackle that large chest? If it contains what I think, we'd best throw it over the side and be rid of it."

We assented, and had no great difficulty—the large chest had not been locked, though it was corroded shut. Presently we cracked it open, and I threw in the light of the electric torch. There was nothing inside except a few skulls and a lot of bones. Maillot laughed.

"I thought as much—most of the slaves who actually laid away the gold, were put in with it." He reached over and picked up a skull. "Look at that gash! Probably Ishmael's diamond-encrusted scimitar did that—he usually attended to his own executions in person. Well, dump it over. We'll leave it to be found tomorrow, and it'll provoke a great mystery and many stories in the newspapers."

It is queer how men react to the sight of gold. I took one of the sovereigns to keep as a curiosity, and the sight of the yellow mass gave me no further interest; the fact that these other chests were undoubtedly filled with coin as well, hardly stirred my pulses. The historic associations connected with all this money were vastly more exciting than the stuff itself—besides, I was still thinking about Tom Keyes.

Maillot, on the other hand, was steaming inwardly, and only by an effort did he keep himself under control, as the avid gleam in his eyes betrayed. El Gezar was under no such inhibitions. He flung himself at the gold, ran it through his hands, panted hoarsely, filled his pockets, and in general behaved as men are supposed to behave at sight of treasure trove; it was, as a matter of fact, a rather bestial procedure.

We hove the brass chest with its grisly contents into the field, and lashed down the tarpaulin over the other chests, then took counsel. We had passed Kemisset, and by taking a road ahead that cut off to the left, El Gezar would not have to go to Rabat at all, but could head straight for the Atlas. Maillot saw the wisdom of this course, and accordingly shook hands with us, promising to send the flivver on to Helal when and as repaired.

"With your papers, you'll have no trouble," he assured El Gezar. "Your pass is signed by the sultan personally, so go ahead, and Allah prosper you!" He pressed my hand warmly. "All luck attend you, my friend; stay as long as you like, and make yourself at home in Helal—the place is entirely at your disposal."

"Thanks," I said. "I'll drop you a line in a day or two."

He broke into a laugh. "I'm afraid the post isn't very regular up there, but you'll be able to send out letters or messages whenever you like. Au revoir!"

I climbed up beside El Gezar, Maillot chucked my bag in back with the chests, and we were off.

And while we bounced and jounced over the rutty road I had

plenty of time to do some tall thinking. Maillot, I had plenty of chance to observe before I had him down pat.

I F I had cherished any illusions in regard to the character of Gayland Brown, the Butcher, this night ride into the dawn would have stripped them away clean. The sight and touch of this gold, the heading back into the hills where he was absolute master, the exultation of having Ishmael's treasure aboard, made him like a drunken man. Perhaps he thought, too, that he no longer needed to wear a mask with me.

He was all one could expect of a renegade. He bawled out bawdy songs in French and English, told stories from his past which would have brought a blush to the most hardened cheek in Sodom, and generally comported himself with all the lusty vigor that was in him. He waxed confidential about his domestic relations up at Helal, where I gathered that he patterned himself upon old Ishmael, who had left a thousand or more children; and promised me my pick of any Berber ladies whom I might fancy. When I suggested that the hillmen might object, he roared with laughter.

"Object? I'd like to see the bloody fools try it!" he cried out. "No, no, my lad, they're dashed well trained, believe me! Oh, you'll see; we'll have a time of it up there, we will!"

So he raved on, until toward daylight he quieted down. He was sleepy, in fact—he had absorbed a tremendous amount of cognac the previous evening.

Despite the moonlight, I saw little of the country; we were rolling across the *bled,* the great upland plain that runs down from the Atlas, and before dawn came we were among the hills. The road was plain bad road, and El Gezar drove like a fiend, so that all I could do was to hang on from bounce to bounce, while the country flitted past in the waning moonlight, with only the occasional thatch-huts of farming Arabs to show human occupancy.

A dozen times during this ride, I was sorely tempted; half a dozen times my hand crept to the pistol in my pocket. Nothing would have been easier than to chuck out this blond animal and then shoot him when he came for me. Here I had the treasure of Ishmael under my hand, a truck to transport it in, and El Gezar had all necessary papers to see me to Marrakesh or beyond. And with him out of the way, any revolt would be nipped in the bud. It was a splendid chance—

But was it? After all, Solomon's purpose would not be served; he was not particularly interested in wiping out El Gezar. What he did want above all things was to implicate Maillot and any of his Arab friends possible—to drag them out of their holes and force them to show what they really stood for. He wanted to discover, too, just what the castle at Helal might hold in the way of munitions. I could be of vastly more service if I played the game properly than if I plumped a bullet into this renegade Briton and made off with a load of gold.

So, to my sorrow, I held my hand when I had the chance, and instead, devoted myself to talk of downtrodden peoples and the civil abuses in Morocco and so forth; I had heard enough radical talk to spout it forth without an effort. A hint or two as to El Gezar's exploits with Krim's army was enough; he would show the bloody French as he had shown the Spaniards, and the frog-eaters would find out what it meant to go up against automatic rifles in the hands of men who knew how, and so on ad lib.

"I say," exclaimed El Gezar suddenly, after a long period of silence, "who is this French woman who first tipped off Maillot to the treasure? According to him, she's a bit of all right."

"She's all right, as far as any woman goes," I returned. "I'm off all of 'em for life, Arab or French."

"Where is she—at Marrakesh?"

"Yes. She was at the Dar ben Daoud, last I heard. Why?"

El Gezar slapped his thigh delightedly. "Not half bad! I'll send her word to come up here and see her blasted treasure; if she wants some of it, she can have it. What?" His elbow dug me in the ribs. "We need a likely female about the place—one that's not tattooed with tribal marks. A ripping idea!"

I said nothing, for fear I would say too much and lose my temper. Just then we sighted our immediate destination, and I thought El Gezar had forgotten his brilliant idea.

The false dawn was gone and the true dawn had brightened from gray obscurity into clear daylight. Our road was following the course of a wide valley, and ahead of us, at a cross-road, appeared a little farm, stage station, estaminet and tavern. The farm, like all the old establishments in country apt to be raided at any time, was a big square walled structure to one side and the estaminet was a spanking new little French outfit, most attractive. It also served as post office for this district, as I noted when we drew up in front.

We piled out stiffly. A greasy Frenchman showed up, followed by a native woman and a train of half-caste children; El Gezar was apparently well known, for we were ushered inside and preparations were made to feed us. My companion talked in Arabic with the proprietor and then went off with him into another room, leaving me at the table; they came back together, laughing.

"Where do we go from here?" I inquired, as El Gezar sank into a chair opposite me.

"We'll keep going until afternoon—I want to get through a couple of villages where there will be soldiers, and we must pass one of the forts later. The blasted frog-eaters won't bother us, however. This afternoon we'll reach the end of the road for this truck and load—it will have to come on empty, for we want it at the farms. We'll have to ship the stuff on in a couple of wagons to get through the pass; there are some bad places there. You and I will take to the saddle for a change—do us good, what? We'll get some sleep this afternoon and go up through the pass after moonrise. Tomorrow morning we'll be at the castle. It's only a fifteen-mile stretch but it takes time. What was that French-woman's name—Pontois, wasn't it?"

"Yes, Jeanne Pontois," I said thoughtlessly, then jerked myself up. "Why?"

El Gezar broke into a roar of laughter.

"I sent her a message—I say, old chap, it's a brilliant idea, what? Wait till she shows up at Helal, eh?"

"She won't," I said curtly.

"What'll you wager?" He grinned at me and fingered his long yellow mustache, then suddenly broke into laughter again and reaching over the table, gave me a slap on the shoulder like the swing of a bear's paw. "When she gets that telegram from you—"

"From me?" I said. "Why, you infernal—"

He was laughing so hard that he did not even hear what I called him—and it was lucky. A moment later I had myself under control; but this journey of ours nearly came to a halt then and there.

There was no way of stopping that message without having a showdown, and this I did not want at all; so I laughed it off. Jeanne would not come up to Helal in any case—Solomon would take care of that!

CHAPTER XIV

THE COMPACT

THREE DAYS at Hela transported me into another
world. Since the dawn of Berber history in Roman days
the tribes of the Atlas, ruled by their feudal chiefs, had remained
independent. Ishmael had broken their power, but from the
towers of Helal I could see the Tadla peaks, far to the south,
where he had left fifty-eight thousand men dead under Berber
spears. The French alone had reduced these tribes, largely by
confirming the powers of their chiefs and not by force of arms.

The passage hither, by mountain defiles where our horses and
mules perforce must go in single file, by narrow valleys, by deep
gorges and high mountain flanks, showed one reason for this
savage independence. The character of the place itself, of the
men around me, showed other and greater reasons.

Gone beyond those snowy peaks was every evidence of civilization; here the middle ages had come to life again. Helal, or
rather the kasbah, occupied the side of a sharp mountain whose
long flank rolled on up beyond it and merged into snowy peaks
above. Below, on three sides, stretched the little valley with its
stream and its farms. Nestling in the very shadow of the castle,
under its west front, was the small mud-walled village with its
marketplace and mosque.

The kasbah itself was enormous, massive, undecorated, a mass
of almost blank stone wall towering to an astonishing height,
with turrets rising here and there—curious projections at their
tops recalling Sudanese architecture. Within these mighty walls

all the folks for thirty miles around could find refuge; here were barns to hold their grain, with shelter for their flocks and herds, and trickling springs watered the place abundantly. Helal was impregnable, except perhaps against artillery placed higher up on the mountain—but how was artillery to get through the passes, unless the first were conquered?

During most of these three days, El Gezar was absent, riding furiously upon obscure errands or superintending the arrival of the chests, which had to be fetched laboriously by wagon and mule-back along a roundabout trail. I was left to my own devices, free as the air, with a corner room of the castle to myself, two black slaves to wait upon me, and liberty to do anything and go anywhere I pleased.

The amount of life in this far corner of the hills was astonishing, fully explaining how armies of fifty to a hundred thousand men had been repeatedly hurled out of these mountains across the Moroccan plains. The village below was in a continual surge with parties coming and going, sometimes entire tribes appearing with daybreak, tents outspread below to the oleanders of the little river, flocks and herds far-scattered; and with the next morning they would be gone. Here too, passed caravans, for Helal was an important trading point and many merchants were established in the village. From all the Upper Atlas beyond came trains of camels or mules or horses with their burdens.

The people were merry, laughing, cruel—white skins tattooed with tribal marks, women unveiled, weapons anywhere. The kasbah itself was garrisoned by a hundred men, and there were various women's quarters; I was always finding my way barred by some grinning black. There was no admixture of races here, for the Berbers have ever been intolerantly proud of their unmixed blood, and the negroes were distinctly slaves. Except for two tiled courts and a large audience hall, and a garden enclosing a few olive trees, there was nothing decorative about the place. It was for use and for hard service and for defense—nothing else.

Upon the walls were half a dozen ancient brass cannonades, but no modern guns. The garrison carried old rifles. Nowhere did I see any signs of arms or munitions, and I began to think that Solomon's information was all wrong. Then, on the third afternoon of my visit, everything broke loose at once.

A train of narrow little carts had come crawling up the valley trail, drawn by donkeys. I had returned my horse to the stables in the rear of the kasbah, after a canter up valley, and coming around to the main entrance saw the train of carts passing through into the great courtyard. From them were being unloaded large and small crates, stenciled in plain English with the words "Repair Parts" or "Tractor Equipment." I stood staring at them; here was the shipment from that Casablanca warehouse which had caused the death of poor Tom.

Up to me swaggered Si Kalil, a wide-cheeked ruffian who commanded the garrison, and who spoke French.

"M'sieu, do you know where El Gezar went?" he asked, frowning. "Here are two who have come seeking him."

He pointed to two figures just inside the gateway.

I knew nothing about El Gezar and said as much, then went to take a look at the new arrivals. One was a blind man—an old white-bearded man, his eyes closed, who sat on the rump of a travel-weary donkey and fingered the beads of a large Muslim rosary, the hood of his *aknif,* or Berber *jellab,* drawn up over his head. Squatting against the gateway beside him was an Arab stripling, evidently his guide. A number of the garrison were gathered around, and Si Kalil joined me with word that the blind man was a saint, one El Meknezi by name, who had lately returned from the Mecca pilgrimage. The guide had so informed them, adding that his master sought El Gezar with word from the cities of the plain.

"He looks done up," I said. "Why not make him comfortable?"

Si Kalil brightened at this, had a mat brought out, and helped the saint descend, offering him food and drink. A ragged holy man from the village below appeared, and I gathered that he was anything but pleased to see a new saint show up out of nowhere. He squatted down opposite the blind man, and began firing questions at him. It was highly amusing to all, especially as the graybeard seemed to get the better of the argument. Si Kalil, grinning, said that he was telling about Mecca and its holy places.

They sat about and hurled rapid-fire conversation at one another in native dialect. I didn't understand a single word that was uttered, but from time to time I seemed to sense a part of the meaning.

"BE CAREFUL—DO not laugh at him!" said a voice in French at our elbow. We turned, and saw the stripling guide standing there. "El Meknezi is a prophet, and it is not well to laugh at saints!"

"By Allah," said Si Kalil, losing his grin, "I was not laughing at him! If he is a prophet, then let him foretell the day of my death. Ask him for me."

"Ask him yourself," retorted the Arab youth. "Why did Allah give you a tongue?"

Si Kalil shoved forward into the throng, and the stripling met my steady gaze.

"So it is you, Hassan!" I said, low-voiced. No others were near us; everyone was intent upon the dialogue between the two saints. "Who's your blind friend yonder?"

His alert eyes laughed at me. "A messenger to El Gezar from Hajj Muhammad—I came as his guide, in order to get word with you. All is well?"

"With me, yes," I returned. "Tell me—how did M. Keyes get killed?"

"He was not killed," said Hassan. "He was shot twice through the body and is in the hospital at Casablanca, but he will not die. He was too inquisitive."

I drew a deep breath. Tom Keyes not dead—this was great news! But this was no time for conversation; Hassan asked where my quarters were located, and promised to show up in the course of the evening. Solomon, he said, was well, and Miss Pontois was in Casablanca looking out for Tom at the hospital.

With this, he slipped away and was lost in the throng, which had swelled rapidly. Voices were lifting eagerly; the local saint, discomfited, withdrew from the contest and Si Kali and his men surrounded the blind graybeard. Looking on, I gathered that he was telling fortunes or something of the sort, to one after another. Si Kalil, scowling blackly, drew out of the crowd and joined me, muttering and pawing his beard.

"That man is a wizard!" he said to me in French. "Saint or not, I would like to take a whip to his back! Dead in three days— hm!" He spat angrily. "Allah upon him!"

Evidently the big rascal had received unwelcome auguries. However, at this instant a shout arose and the men scattered; El Gezar was spurring his jaded horse up the slope to the gate.

He was a handsome devil, for he wore pure white robes—not the horrible ungainly garments of the town Arab, but the fine Berber garments made for horsemen—and carried a splendid silver-sheathed dagger slung across his shoulder by a scarlet band.

"The last of the treasure will be here in half an hour," he said to me. "Hello—I say, what's up? Who's this chap?"

"Some holy man, according to Si Kalil," I replied. El Gezar strode over to the old blind saint, and after a few words turned in a fury upon his men, bellowing forth orders. At once the blind El Meknezi and his guide were led away to suitable quarters, and El Gezar then summoned Si Kalil and gave him detailed instructions which were incomprehensible to me. I could see that my host was both excited and in a high good humor. Presently he turned and beckoned to me.

"Come along—I haven't had a bite to eat since morning, and I'm starved. There's work ahead, too. I say, Smith—you haven't seen any rebels, what?"

"Not a sign of one," I rejoined, following him into the kasbah. We settled down on some cushions in the inner court, where vines draped the pillars and orange-trees, surrounded the central pool, and slaves brought food for him and a cold drink for me.

"Well, just how much is your American bluff worth?" he asked, his pale gray eyes staring at me fixedly. I sensed that some sort of a crisis was crowding me closely. "Suppose you were to learn that actual revolution here in Morocco was imminent—that arms and munitions were ready, that some of the biggest men in the country were ready to rise, with their tribes behind 'em—eh. Would you be inclined to take a shot at the game yourself, or not? Mind, it'll be no child's play. It means something like fifty thousand men up in arms all over the country, and there'll be blood spilled."

I lighted a cigarette, with an assumption of coolness I was far from feeling.

"Are you in earnest?" I demanded.

"Absolutely."

I shrugged. "Right! I'm in for it then, with all my heart! That is, provided there's something in it for me."

He could understand this; it was the one thing needed to convince him that I meant what I said. He showed his yellow fangs in a grin.

"One of those chests of gold—take your pick before we open 'em. What?"

"You've bought something," I said, and straightened up. "Now, then, what's the proposition? Are you behind this revolution?"

"Yes." He wolfed his food and nodded at me, his eyes flaming a little. "You're bound to throw in with us, you know, so there's no use beating about the bush. I'm backing it, and you'll be my second in command. We'll show these beggars how to fight, and the frog-eaters will learn something. It's a bargain?"

"Agreed," I said, and he eyed me curiously.

"You're a cool plucked 'un, you Yank!" he said, with an oath. "Pity you don't speak the lingo; but we'll arrange for that. Tomorrow morning you'll see something; things will happen, understand? We can talk about details then. Ever hear of a holy man called Hajj Muhammad?"

"I've heard something about him, yes," I replied. "Isn't he a saint?"

"Absolutely the best saint in Morocco," and El Gezar guffawed. "He's thick as thieves with a number of the southern chiefs. This blind rascal who came today is a messenger from him. If all is as I expect and hope, this Hajj Muhammad will agree to join me here and bring a picked force of about five thousand men—most of 'em with experience in the army. I'll know definitely after I've talked with that old duffer. If these chaps arrive, they'll come in various parties and meet here; and you'll take command of them."

"I will?"

"Just that. They'll jump at the chance to have a leader who can take 'em in hand properly, whether he's a Christian or not."

"Does Maillot know about all this?"

El Gezar remembered in time that Maillot was to be kept out of it, where I was concerned.

"He? Not much."

"All right. Count me in, old chap," I said with enthusiasm. "And what about that gold?"

"We'll go over that stuff tonight, Smith—open up the chests and stow away the brass, just you and I. Well, I must go see that blind rascal now," and he rose. "By the way, we should have some pleasant company in two or three days."

"Yes? Who?"

"The Frenchwoman—Pontois." He grinned at me. "I sent a couple of men to fetch her here, as soon as we arrived; forgot to tell you about it. I was afraid my telegram might not bring her soon enough. Well, cheerio! See you later."

He swung away, chuckling to himself.

I STAYED sitting right there, gripped by cold fear and anger. I could see now that this big brute had all the time had his heart set on getting hold of Jeanne Pontois—perhaps Maillot had described her beauty, perhaps it was plain devil's instinct. If he had sent two men after her, they would have to trace her from Marrakesh to Casablanca—

As though in response to my half-formed thought, I saw the figure of Hassan crossing the court, and I called to him. He came and joined me, grinning. He was thoroughly enjoying his adventure, and was of course entirely safe—even had it been known that he was the prospective sultan whom these men hoped to place upon the throne.

"Sit down and talk, quickly!" I commanded him. "What message have you for me?"

He looked confused. "None, *m'sieu*—except to obtain a report—"

"Very well. Is Hajj Muhammad sending men here as he promised El Gezar?"

"Yes. Also, he is coming himself. But that will be to destroy El Gezar and not to help him."

"Good!" I exclaimed, vastly relieved. "El Gezar thinks I am an ally, and has promised to give me command of those men."

Hassan grinned at this. I located a stub of pencil and at my request, he drew a notebook from under his *jellab*, and I wrote my message while we talked.

"It is imperative that you leave here at once, tonight," I said, "and get this message to Captain Maillot at Rabat. From there, telephone to the hospital where Keyes was taken; get in touch with him or with Miss Pontois. Tell her that El Gezar has sent men to carry her away, and warn her to be careful. You understand?"

Hassan looked startled. "But the Butcher has women enough! What does he want with her?"

"Ask of Allah, who knows more than I," was my response. "Telephone Solomon, if you can reach him, the same thing. Then report to him what you have seen here. You followed that shipment from Casablanca, I presume?"

Hassan chuckled. "Yes—El Meknezi and I came with it."

"Good work. Remember, it's imperative that this message

should reach Maillot at once. Who are the chief Arabs associated with him—the men around the sultan?"

"Well, there is Said el Wazani, and Si Alem el Idrisi—"

That was enough. I hastily finished my note, and then read it over; it was in English, so there was no danger of Hassan reading it or spoiling my play:

> "Maillot:
>
> Here is the report you wanted; it is bad, I'm afraid. Fighting has broken out between two tribes. El Gezar has been shot and may not live. He says to tell you to bring either Said el Wazani or else Si Alem and get here as quickly as possible. Send word in advance. I have taken charge of things at Helal and may keep all quiet until you arrive. El Gezar says to tell you also that the shipment of tractor parts arrived safely. In haste,
>
> H. Smith."

I folded it up and shoved it at Hassan. "There you are. Need money?"

"No, I have plenty, *m'sieu*," he said, frowning in perplexity. "But perhaps I should wait here until—"

"Get off, and get off tonight and pause for nothing!" I snapped at him. He shrugged resignedly, tucked away the note, and rose with his cheerful smile. "Very well, *m'sieu*. Adieu!"

He disappeared, and I sought my own room, rather relieved than otherwise.

El Gezar had rather forced my hand by imparting his scheme to carry off Jeanne, for that meant swift and sharp action: but, on the contrary, by becoming his second in command I could then carry out the plan I had formed. The keynote of this plan was the presence of Maillot, here in Helal—and that accomplished, the whole game would be won.

I did not see El Gezar again until we met for dinner, in the alcove at one side of the main courtyard. By native custom, no women shared his meals; but tonight he had Si Kalil and another native of some rank from the surrounding country as table companions, and he was in high good humor.

"In three days our five thousand men will be here—and you'll have your legion!" he exclaimed, nudging me—little dreaming that I knew more about that force of men than he did. He then informed the two Arabs what they had perhaps already suspected; namely, that I was joining the conspiracy, and was to become his second in command. He winked at Si Kalil and told him to so inform the garrison in the morning. From his mysterious air, I had already guessed that he was going to spring some big surprise when morning broke; but he would say nothing further about it.

The three of them, as I could gather from the names used, discussed the blind El Meknezi and also Hajj Muhammad, and all three appeared to be exultant over the news today had brought. It was significant that they had no hesitation in speaking freely before the slaves who brought in and carried away the dishes. When the *couscousu* had gone and the mint tea was poured, El Gezar, who seldom touched the concoction, rose and beckoned me.

"All right, Smith," he said in English, with a wink. "Let's go and have a look-see at those chests, what? I ordered some tools put in the room with them. Si Kilal and his lieutenants will be along later to have a look and spread the news. Ishmael's treasure is here, and word of it has already spread far and wide, but no one's seen it yet."

H E L E D the way to one of the inner rooms, whose small window overlooked the great courtyard of the castle, where a thousand men could drill easily. At his order a slave brought two lighted lamps, then he unlocked the door with a massive key and we entered. Piled up before us were the iron-bound chests of Ishmael; the one we had previously opened was roped together. The room was a large one, bare except for a large Glaoua carpet spread out at one side; its bright colors and odd geometrical designs softened down by the lantern-light. El Gezar, with his dagger, cut the rope that bound the smashed chest together, and motioned me to catch hold.

"Empty it on the carpet, and one is out of the way!" he cried, and we dumped the rolling gold pieces in the center of the carpet. Then, laughing, El Gezar waved his hand.

"Take your pick of the chests, as I promised; you can have it taken to your room unopened," he commanded. "Then we'll go at the job—it'll warm us up, what? The nights are brisk, in the Atlas, and no mistake."

I indicated one of the chests, and we shoved it aside, then fell to work with hammers and chisels. The way El Gezar had picked up that first chest and dumped it, with me pretending to help, had been a revelation of the strength of his arms and back; by way of comparison, I took the next when we had smashed into it, and managed the feat myself before he could lend a hand— but it nearly finished me. He stood off and chuckled.

"Not bad by half, Yank!" he said. "You'll do, you will. Now, into them!"

And into them we waded, with hammer and sledge and chisels. During the next half hour the pile of gleaming gold-pieces on the big carpet grew wider and higher, and under the spell of the yellow metal, El Gezar became little short of a madman. There was, indeed, a mad streak in him, which the sight of the treasure brought to the surface.

At length we had finished it—panting, perspiring, disheveled, and dead tired. There before us was heaped English, French and Spanish gold, and that of other countries which today had no name. His gray eyes all ablaze, El Gezar waved his hand at the mass.

"Look at it!" he cried out exultantly. "Ishmael's treasure, slave ransoms from all of Europe, the hoarding of sixty years—and what will it do? It'll chuck the Christians out of Morocco after two hundred years of lying underground, no less! A tenth part of that will be enough to buy over every chief in the country."

I shrugged. "It's nothing to me. If this revolution does break out—"

"You'll see in the morning, my lad!" He swung close to me,

dashed sweat from his eyes, and glared into my face. "Revolution? Hell's bells—it's more than that! It's the loot of every French town in Morocco, understand? It's a rising, not a war; a rising that'll sweep the frog-eaters clean! Now what do you say about it?"

"Nonsense!" I returned, stifling my desire to plant a fist in his face. His mask was off now with a vengeance. "What are you going to do—shoot this money from guns?"

He broke into harsh, wild laughter.

"I'll tell you what I'm going to do, old chap!" he cried out. "I'm going to give all this gold to the Frenchwoman who wanted it—give it to her, let her wallow in it—"

He must have read things in my face. He swung away from me with a sudden leap, flung open the door, and let out a bellow for Si Kalil. Presently the Arabs were staring at the heap of gold, fingering it, slipping odd coins into their pockets, while El Gezar shouted at them in hoarse exultancy, and their growling voices answered.

I went to bed, and left them there.

CHAPTER XV

MASSED MEN

WHEN I wakened in the morning, and remembered the events of the preceding night, I had a feeling of disgust, as though I had been dealing with madmen. The impression of El Gezar's powerful personality was strong upon me; his utterly unreasonable character, his bursts of wild passion, his venomous hatred toward his own people, marked him more clearly than ever as a wild beast, dangerous to all around him.

My room was fitted up in French Victorian style, so to speak, with a wash-stand and bureau. I poured some water and prepared to shave—and opened my toilet kit to find a sheet of paper inside. At the top of the sheet was embossed in red the Seal of Solomon; and below this were a few lines of writing in a beautiful, minute copperplate hand that almost seemed engraving, so perfect was it:

> "Mr. Smith: You're doing very well, but Mr. Keyes is out of it, so I'll depend on you to take his place. Watch out for a French Intelligence officer named Tellier, who will reach Halel in a day or two; he calls himself the horsedealer Ishak. Trust him. Remember, the chief thing is to get Maillot."

How had this note reached me? How long had it been lying in my toilet-case? Certainly it had not been there the previous morning. Hassan had not put it there—he would have given it to me. The obvious conclusion was that Solomon had some other agent here; perhaps the old blind saint.

I laughed grimly as I tore the note into tiny fragments and

scattered them. A lot it mattered what Solomon was doing; the game was out of his hands now, and in mine! Hajj Muhammad would come, and would see for himself that Maillot was backing this affair—then there was this Intelligence officer. Yes, things were fitting in very well indeed.

Four men arrived, bearing my chest of gold, which I had forgotten, and bidding me come at once to join El Gezar. One of them guided me, by passages and stairways, until we came out suddenly on the twenty-foot platform between the two central towers, high over the kasbah gateway. There I found an awning spread, and there, at a table close to the parapet. El Gezar awaited me—he was clad now in a khaki uniform, bare of insignia, a Sam Browne belt holding a pistol at his hip.

"Welcome!" and he waved a hand at the table, which bore fruit and a coffee-urn. "Breakfast is here—and something else is yonder below us. I promised you a surprise this morning, what? You'll have it soon now!"

I had it already, when I stood at the parapet and looked out. The valley below, instead of showing olive trees and oleanders and a few grazing flocks, was now dark with tents which had appeared overnight—tents, and masses of men, swarms of them, their bright garments all aglow in the morning sunlight. Dust was rising along the valley, as far as I could see.

"Who are they?" I asked in astonishment. El Gezar fingered his long mustache and laughed.

"Hillmen—wild uncouth Berbers!" he answered, with a mockery I did not comprehend. "Certain of the chiefs arrive today to receive instructions, and five thousand men are here to greet them fittingly. Some of the chiefs are arriving now. They'll join us here, after a bit. Look at the tribesmen yonder; think you they can smash the squares of Spahis and Tirailleurs and the black Senegalese?"

"I doubt it," I said, looking out at the vast stretch of tents among the trees, where masses of men surged and swarmed.

"You know well enough what chance these untrained hillmen have of standing against regular troops."

El Gezar roared with laughter which I was far from understanding, and was in high good humor as we turned to the table. This stone platform, commanding the valley on one side and the great courtyard of the castle on the other, had been fitted up with the large round Moroccan stuffed seats, and tables stood about bearing cigarettes, dates and little cakes. We applied ourselves to breakfast, and before we had finished, the first of our guests arrived—two handsome elderly men, attired in superb robes, followed quickly by a third. El Gezar introduced me to them but beyond saying that they were mountain chiefs, passed over their names. None spoke French.

Suddenly El Gezar rose, placed a whistle to his lips, and blew a shrill blast. He pointed, and we went to the parapet over the castle courtyard. There, to my astonishment, I saw that the entire garrison had changed costume; gone were robes and rifles, and in their place were trim khaki uniforms and side-arms, with caps of officers. Si Kalil shouted orders, and the whole hundred men fell into swift formations.

"Each of these men becomes a *kaid-el-mia*, a captain of a hundred," said El Gezar, at my elbow. "Make yourself comfortable—this is a long process, Smith."

After that first signal, everything was left in the hands of Si Kalil below, who gave all the orders; evidently this show for the benefit of the chieftains had been carefully prearranged. The hundred officers now split up into various parties and most of them vanished into the vast recesses of the castle, leaving only Si Kalil and a dozen more in the courtyard. The morning was cold, and at one side, in the sunlight, I saw the white-bearded figure of the blind saint, fingering his rosary as he warmed himself. The disappearance of his guide, clearly, had attracted no attention or remark.

Two of the officers from below joined us, saluted briskly, and then stood at one side as though awaiting orders. El Gezar told me they were the sons of one of our guests, then drew us all to the other side of the platform. And here we witnessed the beginning of an extraordinary scene—one which showed what this blond El Gezar had been doing with his time besides managing farms.

THE THOUSANDS of hillmen in the valley below were drifting up to the kasbah gateway and then turning sharply aside to reach a small gate on the north side of the castle, where they were pouring into the kasbah in a steady, slow-moving swarm. This unbroken stream, this solidly moving mass of men, gradually drew out into a column of fours, winding up the approach and vanishing in the maw of the high stone walls like an unending snake.

Two more chiefs came riding up to the entrance on superb horses, dismounted, and were brought up to join us. In the midst of the greetings, one of our guests gave a sharp ejaculation.

"Wallah!"

We followed his stare, looking down now into the great courtyard of the palace. And, abruptly we received the first inkling of what was really going on down below, in the recesses of the enormous castle.

A steady stream of men was pouring from the castle into the courtyard—the same men who had come in by the side entrance, but no longer the same. Gone were the flowing robes, the ragged jellabs; in their place were trim khaki tunics, uniforms, caps, cartridge bandoliers; fingering glittering rifles or hastily adjusting belts, the men came pouring forth. And as they came, they fell swiftly into ranks that moved forward and halted again, full companies of men, commanded by the garrison officers, with lieutenants and sergeants from among their own ranks. About it all was an amazing precision that bespoke training. There was no confusion, but each man knew his place and fell into it.

"Well?" said El Gezar triumphantly to me, amid the admiring comments of the staring chiefs. "What about it now, Smith? How do you like these raw, uncouth Berbers, eh?"

"You've done wonders!" I exclaimed. "This drill isn't military training, though—"

He broke into laughter, then pointed down. "Watch! You haven't seen anything yet."

Si Kalil, below, barked out an order. The ranks of men were now filling the whole courtyard; swiftly, moving like clockwork figures, they began pouring forth from the gateway of the castle and moving down to the valley beyond. And ever as they poured forth, into the courtyard continued that constant stream of men who had just changed and armed, and who fell into new ranks taking the places of those marching out.

It was a marvelous thing to see, this miracle of unending swarms of raw hillmen pouring in at one gate and coming out at another in uniform. El Gezar was fiercely exultant, as well he might be; and now, with a sharp word, drew our attention to a new company forming up. This was composed of men who wore steel helmets—and I noted that they were of the French pattern, which was significant of Maillot's hand—and who carried, not rifles, but the machine or automatic rifles which had just arrived.

Company after company of these ranks formed up, until the courtyard was filled with them; a full regiment, I estimated. Then they began to march out after the others, who had fallen into rank on the open ground below, two regiments of them.

I turned to El Gezar. "How have you kept this secret?" I asked, curious to know the way he had managed it. "Here there is a constant stream of travelers, pilgrims, merchants; have none of them ever witnessed this force in the making?"

"No," he said. "This is the first time we have carried it out by daylight. Besides, we keep watch on the passes, never fear! Those who come into this country are known—and even so, we trust them with no secrets. Spies may be anywhere. Now, however, it matters little what rumors go forth. Here come the machine-guns."

Grunts of delight and admiration broke from the watching chiefs around us. More steel helmets were flooding into the courtyard below, and with them were coming mules from the stables in the rear. We saw machine guns carried out, swiftly taken apart, packed for transport, and led forth in an apparently endless procession; I counted a hundred and forty guns in all. And after them, again, came more rifle-armed companies.

All this took time, of course; we sat there for hours, while from below us came the steady tramp of feet, the sharp barking of orders, the odors of rising dust and of sweat. The regiments waiting down below in the sunlight had stacked arms, awaiting the arrival of the full force.

El Gezar sat down beside me on the parapet, and lighted a cigarette.

"Well?" he said, his pale gray eyes watching me. "You don't know the half of it yet; when you hear the campaign outlined, you'll realize a few things. But what do you think of my five thousand, eh? What do you think will happen when they strike the French?"

"As I recall," I answered slowly, "there are four thousand Senegalese encamped near Meknez alone."

He chuckled. "And do you know, also, that black troops cannot stand before Arabs? Fact. The Senegalese have an hereditary fear of these hillmen."

"It's a minor point," I said. "You forget the aviation camps. One big bombing plane would take care of your whole army."

"If it remained an army, a single entity, yes!" El Gezar beckoned one of the two aides and issued orders; the aide saluted and departed. "Aviation camps! Do you know what will take care of them? I'll show you, my lad. Parties of a dozen men each, with little playthings like this, striking the aviation camps at Taza and Fez and so on at the same hour—"

The aide returned. From him El Gezar took a small, light grenade, drew the pin, and hurled it along the parapet. It burst; fragments of glass glittered in the air, and over the stones ran streams of blazing fire. So, he had incendiary bombs as well!

Finally the stream of men came to an end, and as the last of them marched out, we saw a ragged, half-naked shape riding upon a mule, with two followers shuffling along behind, coming up the valley. El Gezar caught up a pair of binoculars.

"Hajj Muhammad!" he exclaimed, with an exultant oath.

The name provoked a stir among the chiefs. They craned forward to see, broke into sharp talk, and showed excited interest. It was plain enough that all I had heard about the holiness of the *hajj* was true. But—what would his arrival bring forth? Was Tellier with him?

By this time, midday was at hand. A thin, clear call rose into the air from the minaret of the village mosque, below. It quavered and lifted, rose and fell again; and I saw a remarkable thing. Hajj Muhammad, who was by this time nearing the gateway, halted his mule, dismounted, and knelt in the dust with his two men. The regiments yonder in their ranks swayed forward upon their faces. The chiefs around me, and El Gezar himself, and the watching throng of villagers below, went through the prescribed formula of ablutions with dust or sand, and the sound of their voices arose in a great singsong wave. Even the blind saint and the slaves down in the courtyard followed suit. I was the only man who remained on my feet.

At length it was ended, and Hajj Muhammad came on to the entrance. He was not the type of holy man who enshrines sanctity in opulence: he was just as tattered, dirty, wild-eyed as when I had seen him first. He strode into the courtyard, and his voice crackled out; the blind El Meknezi came to his feet, and two saints embraced one another.

Five minutes later, Hajj Muhammad joined us on the platform, and gave the chiefs his saintly blessing. He shot one look at me, and spat, and made a remark which was obviously offensive—it was part of his role to detest all Christians. El Gezar's reply evidently pacified him, and he accepted a seat.

I sized him up covertly, out of the corner of my eyes, as he sat dourly and glumly without saying a word.

THE NOON meal was served us here in the cool shade beneath the awning, amid a flow of most energetic conversation. I was distinctly out of it, for El Gezar was too busy with the saint to give me much attention, and I knew no Arabic. However, I could see that Hajj Muhammad was being very affable and playing the somewhat dubious part he had undertaken.

"Want to come along for another look at the treasure?" said El Gezar to me, when the meal drew to its close. "Then we'll return here to watch the maneuvers."

"Hang the treasure," I said. "I'm comfortable, thanks. Are your troops going into camp permanently?"

He shook his head. "Tomorrow morning they'll have vanished again," and he grinned sourly. "Muhammad will have his men here in three days, he says—then you can try your hand. You'll have to make a quick job of it, though; a week from today the bally revolution breaks out."

With which piece of pleasant information, they left me alone on the parapet, all of them filing off to look at Ishmael's gold. They were gone half an hour, and returned with eyes agleam, gold coins clenched in their fingers, and new excitement in their voices—all, that is, except the saint. He remained cold, fierce-eyed, unkempt as ever.

During another hour we sat there watching the regiments in the valley, below, through binoculars El Gezar provided. The drilling, I must admit, was admirable; and the renegade, who thought I knew more about military matters than I did, hung upon my opinion. I flattered him highly, and evidently the others did also. He stood up, fired a shot in the air, and the review was over; the regiments began their march back into the kasbah, and presently the side entrance was erupting wild hillmen, swarming back to their tents among the trees.

We did not watch this slow process, however. A table was brought, and upon this El Gezar spread out several maps—large-scale military maps straight from French headquarters. What now ensued became clear to me from gestures and from occasional words of explanation flung at me by El Gezar: the chiefs talked volubly, but Hajj Muhammad sat like an image, only the blazing eyes in his thin features showing that he understood perfectly.

The infernal genius of El Gezar—or did it come from Maillot through him—appalled me when I comprehended what he had in mind. It was exactly the scheme Solomon had outlined to us at Marrakesh, but infinitely more detailed and perfect. El Gezar's maps showed each concentration of French troops, their supply and munitions dumps, their camp layout.

He proposed to split up his five thousand trained men into companies, scatter them from south to north, and use them as a nucleus about which would gather the forces of the rebel chiefs. Hillmen would flood down, seeping into the towns, and upon a given day there would be a rising as bloody and sudden as the Sicilian Vespers. Given no chance to resist, the various camps would be stormed under a spray of automatic-rifle fire; one or two might hold out, but most of them must fall.

"And the sultan?" queried Hajj Muhammad grimly.

"The sultan will be Mulai Hassan—upon whom be peace!"

There was some discussion about Hassan; no one, I gathered, knew just where he was, and I chuckled to myself. Hajj Muhammad suspected I knew, for his eyes pierced into me and I caught a glimmer in them as of a laugh held back; but he said nothing.

There, then, was El Gezar's fine scheme; and when he had talked with the chiefs, he told me with a grin that he would have thirty thousand men in the field inside two days from the time he called them out, and that another three days would find a hundred thousand men in arms. In this he may have been correct, though he did not know that the allegiance of Hajj Muhammad to his plan was more than doubtful.

I left them sitting there, ordered a horse, and went for a gallop up the valley to get away from it all. The thought of French colonists and troops shot down in a wild wave of massacre was sickening; blood and fire breaking over the French towns and hamlets, looting and destruction, murder and slavery—primitive wild beasts destroying an entire new civilization! And not for liberty either, but to further the aims of a few unscrupulous devils who were using the weapons of intrigue and power for purely selfish ends—knowing that France must inevitably stamp out Morocco as a nation in consequence.

Much was to happen—and did.

CHAPTER XVI

THE SPY

WITH THE French army away down in the mountains near the Algerian border, caught there, the passes blocked, communications cut off—it might well be that the rest of Morocco would fall before the onslaught! These drilled regiments we had seen were imposing, and the sight of them lingered impressively; even Hajj Muhammad had showed how deeply this realization had gone into him. As Solomon had said, one spark amiss might fire a whole train of destruction.

There on that ride, with the snowy peaks around, I settled on my plan. It was a desperate one, and yet it promised success—if all went well. I came back to the castle at sunset, and found the tents in the valley gone. By all the trails, that assemblage of five thousand men was seeping away and vanishing. And, entering the castle, I found the chiefs departed also, gone home to tell of what they had heard and seen, and to gather their tribes of fighting-men. Of them all, Hajj Muhammad alone remained, squatting in the courtyard with his two followers at his side, while nearby sat the blind El Meknezi fingering his beads. The garrison of the kasbah had resumed their native attire, also.

I went up to Hajj Muhammad and asked abruptly if either of his two followers spoke French.

"I understand it a little, *sidi*," answered one of them, while the saint's fierce eyes rested upon me in a steady, questioning glare.

"Then ask the *santon* when his men will arrive here."

"Not before two or three days," came the answer, after the question was put.

"In case I need some of them before then, can he get them?"

"Only Allah knows," was the translated response. I repressed an oath and turned away.

THERE WAS a wild party that night, the villagers flocking up from below and bringing some sheep which were butchered and cut up; there was plenty to eat, raw hill wine to drink, for these Berbers drank regardless of religion, and interminable dancing. It was not the slinking dance of Arabs, but wild and rapid jigging of a sort peculiar to Berbers, and vastly interesting. El Gezar had a private celebration of his own afoot, and was highly affronted when I refused to join him, but I went to my own room and so to bed early, with flutes and drums and singing coming to me from outside. And all night I dreamed of stalwart hillmen butchering blacks and Frenchmen—a reflex, I presume, of the average size of the soldiers I had seen. Your Moroccan is far more robust than the average European, and can wear him down and still appear perfectly fresh.

No premonition assailed me when I wakened in the morning; I had slept later than usual, and after breakfasting, left the castle and walked down to the stream in the valley below, for a dip— bathing facilities had been left out when Helal was constructed.

I had figured carefully, by asking various questions, and if Hassan got my message through without any dallying by the wayside, it should reach Maillot sometime today. This meant that Maillot should get here no later than the following morn- ing; he would cover the distance far more rapidly than Hassan. Therefore I could not delay what I proposed to do, longer than this same evening.

So, at least, I thought to myself, as I dressed again after my dip in the icy water, and started back. Then I saw that something had happened at the castle, and hurried my steps. A crowd was trailing up the approach from the village, and thronging about the gates. As I drew closer, I heard a burst of wild shouts, and beside the castle gates saw half a dozen horses, heads drooping to the dust, weary and worn. Who had arrived?

A cry came to me—a sharp, piercing cry in a woman's voice, and my heart leaped. Could it be possible, or was I deceived by that voice? A storm of shouts and yells went up from the hill folk about the gates, and then fell sudden silence. The stentorian bellow of El Gezar lifted loudly, and as though in answer to this, one short, fierce yell arose from the hillmen. Again I heard the woman's cry—this time muffled, but I knew whose voice it was.

I broke a way through the throng clustered there, frantically. As I did so, sharp commands came from the courtyard within, followed by a resounding volley of shots. I burst through the crowd and saw half a dozen of the garrison lined up; and, against one wall, a limp figure that had fallen forward, blue jellab running with blood. El Gezar, his eyes blazing, swung on me.

"Smith! Look there—see what my men caught, would you? A Frenchman, blast him—a spy on his way here, posing as a horse-trader! There's payment for his damned insolence!" His fierce exultancy passed into a grin, and leaning forward, he caught me by the arm. "And what d'ye think, eh? They brought her along—she's inside now!"

"Who?" I demanded.

"The Pontois woman. Looked more like a girl to me—what? We'll investigate, eh?" And he grinned into my face, his eyes bloodshot with passion and triumph. Then he pulled me over to where the body of poor Tellier lay, and kicked it face upward, savagely.

"That's what spies get in Helal!" he cried out. "Look at him, Smith—the damned fool thought he could deceive us! One of my men he had jailed for a year; I've met him myself, during the Riff trouble—and he thought we were bally asses, not to recognize him!"

He swung around, shouting something which brought a yell from the hillmen at the gate, and they came surging into the courtyard. I turned away, knowing that now the crisis was upon me—yes, now I must drop everything and act, swiftly and sharply and mercilessly, even though it spoiled the greater game!

A queer little sound reached me, halted me—through all the uproar. It was exactly like the wheezy chuckle of John Solomon, and so startled was I that I actually looked around to see where the pudgy little man could be. Then I laughed harshly and passed on. Yes, this would be a likely place for Solomon to turn up!

The one thought hammered at me; now I must act, act, act!

CHAPTER XVII

THE FALL OF EL GEZAR

SOMEHOW I got away from it all, got off to myself away from the dust and blood. The last thing I noted was the crowd about the body of Tellier, hacking off the head, hoisting it up to be placed above the gateway. They had caught him, somehow—what matter now?

What mattered anything? Jeanne was inside these walls; my warnings had gone out too late, if indeed Hassan had got them out at all as yet. I could still hear her wailing cry as she had been plucked from her horse and carried inside, probably with a vision of hell on the way.

"Damn it!" I said to myself. "That's what comes of having a woman in the game; they're always raising hell with everything and knocking careful plans to bits. Thank heaven I'm not in love with her! At least, I can think the business out calmly."

I had to come to her rescue, of course—and after looking into El Gezar's eyes, knew that it must be done soon. The only way I could manage it was by advancing my plan, and striking before I had expected to strike; and it must be done at all costs. Besides, I had endured about all of El Gezar that I could stomach.

So, with my gun in my pocket, I left my room, wishing vainly that I had not returned Maillot his silenced revolver.

I went to the courtyard. Outside the gate, a crowd of villagers were staring up at the grisly head of poor Tellier. His body had vanished, and the courtyard was empty except for Si Kalil and a group of his lieutenants, who were talking with the blind

El Meknezi. The commander turned as he sighted me with a malicious grin.

"Come, *M'sieu l'Americain!* Let this holy man tell your fortune!" he exclaimed.

"Allah upon him!" I rejoined, with one of the few Arabic phrases I knew. "Where is the other one, Hajj Muhammad?"

He shrugged. "Gone to visit the *taleb* of the mosque, who is sick."

"And El Gezar?"

As though in answer, came the frightful scream of a man, and into the courtyard staggered a black slave, holding himself about the middle and streaming blood. He cried out again, and fell headlong; a knife-stroke had disemboweled him. In the doorway behind appeared El Gezar, jets of blood over the white robes he had reassumed, his silver-hafted knife in hand.

"Haul that dog away to join the Frenchmen!" he cried out, then his furious features were composed at sight of me, and he thrust his blade in its sheath. "I say, Smith! Come along and have a drink—then we'll have a look at the lady, what?"

"Right!" I rejoined cheerfully. "But you might make it a bit clearer to these chaps that they're to accept orders from me. They seem to think I'm something of a joke."

This was dangerous business, as I well knew, but I had learned from him, in the past few days, how to handle these men of his. He swung upon them with a furious roar of Arabic, and they hurriedly saluted, casting half-frightened glances at me. Then, as I strode to him, he turned and led me into the passage beyond.

"We'll fetch her into the room where the gold is waiting for her," he exclaimed, with a burst of boisterous laughter. Catching sight of a slave, he gave a bellowed order that sent the black scuttling in panic.

Striding down the corridors ahead of me, he crossed the court where water splashed on the tiles and orange-trees stood about the pool, and so into the passage he sought. By the locked door, a number of slaves were waiting with cushions, a table, and other

burdens. El Gezar unlocked the door, and we were in the great
room with the pile of battered chests at one end, and the heap
of gold on the carpet at the side. The one window, which was
high up, opened upon the castle courtyard.

The slaves, casting sidelong frightened glances at El Gezar,
brought in their burdens, and loaded the table with fruit and
dishes. He caught up a bottle of cognac and poured stiff drinks
into two of the glasses—gorgeous tall Venetian glasses of gold
and crystal, probably some loot of past chieftains—and held
one out to me.

"Luck!"

"Luck!" I echoed, and clinked glasses with him, and put down
the fiery stuff straight.

For a space we were alone together, and I was tempted, but
instead of acting, I lit a cigaret and listened to his mad talk. He
was in a turbulent, furious mood, kicked the gold coins about
the room, strode up and down—then whirled abruptly as steps
came from the passage.

Jeanne stood in the doorway.

A dumpy slave-woman stood either side of her; El Gezar
bawled at them and they scurried away. Then he grinned at
Jeanne and stood fingering his mustache. She came into the
room, her eyes going from one to the other of us, evidently
far from understanding her position; she was very cool, and to
my astonishment her gaze was composed and she even smiled
faintly—until El Gezar took a step forward, caught her by the
arm, and glared into her face.

"So, my pretty one!" he exclaimed, with a guffaw. "Do you see
the gold—Ishmael's gold—the gold you came so far to seek!
There is it before you—you've found it, my lass! Lie in it, eat it,
drink it—and you'll know what gold's worth!"

He shoved her violently as though to fling her aside on the
pile of gold—but she resisted his effort, unfrightened. The
reduced bandages on her arms were scarcely noticeable.

I had quietly stepped to the door, which was closed. On the

inside was a heavy bar of wood, and this I dropped into place, then turned. To my astonishment, Jeanne was giving him look for look, a high, proud anger in her face.

"Are you a man or a brute!" she flashed out. "Shame upon you, an Englishman—why, you must be drunk!"

A great guffaw of delight burst from El Gezar.

"Why, here's a woman for you!" he cried. "Englishman be damned! I'm El Gezar the Moor, do you understand? And you're the sort I've been looking for—lie on your gold, girl, lie there and taste of it—"

VIOLENTLY, A burst of mad laughter on his lips, he hurled her headlong upon the gold—and as he did so, my pistol-mouth pressed gently but firmly against his neck. He felt the cold touch and stood paralyzed, his features frozen, his eyes rolling around as his head slowly turned, until he was staring at me there beside him.

"You!" he said hoarsely.

"Exactly," I returned, and with my free hand deftly slid his big knife from its scabbard, and tossed it away. I knew he carried no gun, for he disliked the weight unless he was in uniform and wore a belt. "Now, you sit down—you damned renegade dog, if you make a false move I'll drill you! Sit down."

His empurpled features relaxed in a grin.

"So, my fine recruit, you're showing your true colors, eh?" he exclaimed. "And if I take you by the throat—you'll shoot me, will you?"

"Just so," I returned. "Try it. I only wish you'd give me an excuse to put a bullet into your dirty hide—"

"Stop, stop!" Jeanne's voice rang in upon us both. I did not take my eyes from his, but could see her rising to her feet, arm outstretched. "Smith—do not, do not! You must not shoot him! He does not know what he is saying or doing—"

"The hell he doesn't!" I cut in rudely. "Stop your talk. You're like all the rest of 'em, falling for a big brute and eating up his rough stuff. I've got something better to do than risk my life in this game and have you sticking your head into it, so shut up."

El Gezar laughed a little, and made a slight ironic bow to Jeanne.

"I must apologize for my apparent roughness," he began. "This gentleman has been posing as a friend and associate of mine—"

I used my pistol then and there, but I did not reverse it and hit him with the butt, as the heroes of romance do. I gripped the gun, brought it up, and cracked him over the head with the base of the butt—which is the dirtiest blow possible to give with an automatic pistol.

It was entirely efficient; I was taking no chances on halfway measures. El Gezar crumpled up and fell on his face, and a sharp cry broke from Jeanne.

"Oh—you brute! You've killed him—"

"My lord, *will* you shut up!" I said, looking at her in disgust. "I hope I have finished him, but no such luck. Don't you realize what he intended doing with you? Don't you know he was taking you for one of his women? Don't you savvy that he had you kidnapped and fetched here for that purpose—and that he's promoting a massacre that will burst out all over the country? Now, shut off the sentimental tap and keep quiet. I'm going to save you, if you give me half a chance. There's your fine noble fellow—with the blood of a poor murdered devil all over him still!"

I jerked off El Gezar's blood-spattered white *jellab* and flung it at her feet, and she shrank back, staring at it, probably seeing the stains for the first time.

Taking the silver-hilted dagger, I slit up some of El Gezar's fine white wool garments and trussed him up solidly, then crammed his mouth full and gagged him with other strips. This taken care of, I took his keys and pocketed them, then went over to the table and helped myself to food and fruit and a long drink. Jeanne just stood there staring.

"Sit down and take it easy, Jeanne," I told her. "Eat, drink and be merry, for you may be dead tomorrow. Listen, young lady! I'm sorry if I was rude—"

"You were and you are," she said icily. "I don't pretend to understand what all this is about, and I don't care. I received a telegram signed by your name, and the men who carried me off said they were bringing me to you, and so—"

"And so you show yourself about as reasonable as a woman usually is, eh?" I cut in. She drew herself up and pointed to the door, with a furious gesture.

"Leave me! I prefer the society of this man to yours, do you understand?"

"You bet," I said. "And I've no time to waste on you right now, either. If I can start you off right away with a couple of men, do you want to return to Casablanca?"

Her gaze, cold and hard as ice, searched me doubtfully.

"Certainly," she answered.

"All right, then. Sit tight, and you're safe here—and leave that bird the way he is, if you have any sense," I returned. "You probably can be trusted that far, anyhow. He's the renegade Solomon mentioned—El Gezar."

"I don't believe it," she flashed out.

"Be damned to you, then," I muttered angrily, and turned to the door. "You'd be believing it all right about now, if I hadn't settled him! Anyhow, both of you are safe enough here."

I unbarred the door, went out, and then locked it with El Gezar's keys. It was a huge, massive old door, four inches thick, and only a battering ram could open it by force.

If I had stopped to think of it, Jeanne's attitude was a perfectly natural one. She knew little about me personally, except what Tom Keyes might have told her, and there was no knowing what those men sent by El Gezar had dinned into her ears, or just what he had said in the telegram to which he had signed my name. However, I admit frankly that I was infuriated by her words and manner, and under the circumstances with some reason; also, I do not love arguments with women, and I had more important business on my hands than hanging around trying to persuade her that I was an honest man. It was a good deal simpler to lock her up and attend to other matters first.

"Trust a skirt to gum up a game, every time!" I muttered angrily, as I strode along the passages on my way down to the courtyard. "By all the rules, Jeanne should fall on my neck with joyous tears—but does she? Not much. Instead, she's all for the brute who meant to assault her—huh! I'm going to burn off that yellow mustache first thing I do."

When I reached the courtyard, not a soul was in sight except two guards loafing by the gateway in the shade, and the blind El Meknezi on his mat, also in the shade, and sound asleep. I went to the guards and demanded Si Kalil. They shrugged, waved a hand down the valley, and made me understand that he was not at home.

Hajj Muhammad, then. They understood me right enough, and poured out a long story of which I got only the saint's name. I pointed at the village inquiringly, but they shook their heads and grinned at me, and talked some more.

This blasted matter was growing serious. I knew what I wanted to do, but was entirely helpless, for the only man in the garrison who I knew spoke French, was Si Kalil. Inquiring of this precious pair, I met only with smiling shrugs. Si Kalil was gone, and Hajj Muhammad was no longer in the village, but somewhere else—and I was stumped. I walked over to the blind holy man on his mat; the sound of voices had awakened him, and he had caught up his beads and was mumbling away at the hundred ineffable names of Allah.

"Do you speak French, El Meknezi?" I demanded. "French, understand?"

He shook his head, still cowled with the hood of his burnoose or *jellab*—hard to tell what it was, for the rags and dirt. His gray-bearded face was dirty, also, and his hands had never seen the ablutions of his faith, evidently.

"Yes, you blasted old imitation saint—what you need is for someone to kick you in the pants and put you to work, and Hajj Muhammad the same!" I said in disgust. "If I could get a couple of men to take that confounded girl off my hands and get her started to Casablanca, I'd be all set; but no such luck. I have to wait until Si Kalil gets back. And Hajj Muhammad's gone, and Maillot will get here tonight or in the morning—damn it all!"

IT OCCURRED to me that some of the slaves might know French, and I made my way toward the women's portion of the castle. When I came to a doorway guarded by a black man, who was sitting down enjoying the shade, I tried to make him understand me; two others gathered, and one of the slave women, but none of them spoke a word of French. As though to exasperate me further, one of them grinned and spoke in English.

"Me British subject, Krooboy! Me British subject, Krooboy!"

They were the only English words he knew—probably drilled into him down the west coast when he was a boy, before slavers carried him off and sold him north. At this, I gave it up and made my way back to the treasure-chamber, hot and angry. The sight of poor Tellier's head over the entrance gate, a mass of buzzing flies, had sickened me; and vultures were circling farther down the valley, tokening where the body of Tellier and that of the dead black had been flung.

As I was selecting the huge key that served the door, two men came toward me along the corridor, and I waited. They were two of the chief men in the garrison—I recognized them as officers who had served as captains during the maneuvers. They halted, laughed, and spoke to me, but I could make out nothing. One of them held up a French military pass.

"Casablanca," he said, and repeated the word, then beckoned me down the corridor to the tiled court, where a large window opened on the courtyard. There he pointed to two mules being led up and saddled. "Casablanca!"

"Hello!" I exclaimed. "You're going to Casablanca, is that it?"

They grinned and nodded, and asked for El Gezar. I shook my

head, motioned them to wait here, and went back to the room. There I unlocked the door, and in the nick of time.

Jeanne had El Gezar's big dagger, and was just about to cut him free.

I was not very ceremonious about it. One jump took me into the room, and I caught the knife from her and sent it whirling. She came erect with a blaze of anger in her eyes, but I gave her no chance to speak.

"You're a bigger fool than I took you for, Jeanne," I broke in. "Now, listen to me! A couple of these men are going to Casablanca. You can go with them if you like—and, young lady, you'd better go while the going's good, or you'll never get away! If you're ready, come along."

She changed countenance, as she stared at me.

"Are—are you in earnest!" she exclaimed. "But I thought—"

"I don't give a hang what you thought or what you do," I said, "so long as you get out of here safely. When you reach Casablanca, get in touch with Solomon first thing; but never mind, it will probably be too late. I can handle the rest of the game myself. Here," and I caught up El Gezar's blood-splotched white jellab, "throw this on and come along. The first town you come to, the first Frenchman you see, break away from these two rascals and have them pinched if possible, then get on to Casablanca. Give my regards to Tom and tell him I sure as hell pity him; never mind explanations—he'll know what I mean. Come on!"

I swept her off her feet, and before she quite knew what it was all about, had draped her with El Gezar's jellab and had her out in the hall. The two Arabs were waiting by the window, and grinned at sight of her, nodded, and smiled. I pointed to the mules and held up three fingers, employed all the sign-talk possible, and mentioned Casablanca. They nodded complete understanding and one of them departed, evidently to order up the third mule. With the other one, we went down to the courtyard.

"I—I don't know what to say, Mr. Smith," said Jeanne, half

appealingly. "I'm afraid I made a frightful fool of myself—I should have known you were a friend—"

"Nevermind," I said. "There's the other mule coming for you, and I can only give you my best wishes for a trip that may be unpleasant. Do you want a gun? Here, take mine—let 'em see me giving it to you—that's fine!"

"But, please!" she said, taking the pistol. "You must let me say—"

"Say nothing," I interrupted. "All I want you to do is to get out, and do it quick. You're a fine woman and all that, and I admire you tremendously; but not right now, here in Helal. You are too beautiful for this place. You belong in a finer setting, one more worthy of your beauty and ability; in the arms of the man who loves you. And that's Tom Keyes, unless I miss my guess. Oh, never mind starting and blushing—hello! Here's your mule, a fine big white one fit for the sultan himself—"

I kept up a fine flow of talk and gave her no chance to break in with a word until the third mule was brought up. Then I assisted her into the saddle, while the two grinning hillmen mounted their own animals. They started off.

"Goodby," she called, turning toward me, her face now a little white and frightened. "I—I'm sorry for everything—"

"Goodby and good luck," I returned, with a wave of my hand, and the three of them went ambling away down the descent. I drew a deep breath of relief as I watched them go. A number of the garrison were lounging about, and I caught El Gezar's name; evidently the fact that she wore his white *jellab* puzzled them—which was as I intended.

I STARTED back into the castle, then paused sharply. Was it possible that the blind saint did understand French after all? Had—but no. I had not spoken French before him except to ask the question, therefore he could not have called those two men and told them to go to Casablanca. No, that was nonsense; and a glance showed me that he had fallen asleep once more on his mat, his rosary still clenched in his dirty fingers.

When I regained the treasure-chamber, I found that El Gezar was now conscious, and flinging himself about the floor in frantic efforts to get loose. His face, above the white strips of his gag, was purple with fury, and his terrible cold gray eyes fairly blazed at me. He was making incoherent noises which, naturally, were as futile as his struggles. I chuckled, and poured myself a drink.

"Here's luck, Gayland-Brown-El Gezar!" I said, looking down at him. "You ornery devil, you'll need all the luck you can grab before I'm through with you! Unfortunately I don't feel like shooting you in cold blood—"

Which reminded me that I had nothing with which to shoot. So after making sure his struggles had not loosened his bonds, I locked up El Gezar again and went off to his own quarters, which were not far from mine. On the way I visited the courtyard, made certain Hajj Muhammad had not returned, and went on with a worried feeling. I wanted to get hold of that holy man in the worst way in order to let him know that Maillot was probably coming and that I would need some of his promised men badly. There was no getting him, however.

Further, I wanted to do quite a number of things, all of which were clearly mapped out in my mind. I wanted to make a tour of inspection of El Gezar's munitions and arms, and send out half or more of the garrison on fictitious errands in search of fictitious French spies; but in these and other respects I was absolutely helpless, until Si Kalil came along to act as my mouthpiece. I had overlooked this essential, to my sorrow.

A thorough search of El Gezar's room revealed absolutely nothing except a large and choice collection of Japanese books and French picture cards of the kind that can be bought along the Quai des Augustins in Paris. There was no sign of a weapon—these, obviously, were kept elsewhere. I was balked once more; I wanted a pistol, but could not very well walk up to one of the garrison and take his, as I was determined to do.

By this time, the afternoon was wearing along; and then came the final blow. I went down to the courtyard and was trying to make one of the men understand that I wanted him to go and find Si Kalil, when a commotion arose, shouts resounded, and there was a general commotion in the village below. A number of horsemen appeared on the road, mounting toward the gates, carrying an unconscious figure in their midst; upon closer approach, it proved to be that of Si Kalil himself, his bearded features covered with blood.

From the excited talk and gestures, I understood that he had fallen from his horse, and the animal had kicked him. He was not dead, but he was badly hurt and in no shape to do any talking. I cursed the luck and started for the passage, when I heard something that paralyzed me for the moment.

It was the voice of El Gezar, and it was coming from the little window in the treasure room that opened on the court-yard. Somehow he had worked himself free, and was probably standing there shouting to his men below, trying to make his bellowing roar heard above the noise and confusion.

I went up the stairs on the jump, desperate now—and with good reason.

CHAPTER XVIII

JOHN SOLOMON'S SURPRISE

WHEN I dodged into that room and dropped the bar
of the door behind me, El Gezar had heard me at the
door. He was dropping from his perch on the piled-up treasure
chests under the window. He was free—the cut strips of wool
by the silver-hafted dagger on the floor showed that somehow
he had reached the knife and made use of it.

As he hit the floor, I got to him; neither of us had any time
to dive for the dagger or any other weapon—I had to stop his
mouth before he did any further yelling. I certainly succeeded in
this, for as we crashed together my fist slammed him squarely in
the mouth and we both went sprawling into the corner.

Then there was a fight. It was a pity Jeanne was not there; she
certainly missed getting a liberal education.

El Gezar came up spitting blood and teeth and oaths. He
beat me to my feet and put over a crack to the jaw that laid me
out, then he came in to finish it. He was quick as a flash for
all his size, and had a kick in each fist, and would have settled
Hank Smith then and there—except that I caught his ankle
and upset him.

With that, we were into it hammer and tongs, tooth and
toenail; and I don't mean maybe. We were down and up repeatedly, and so rapid was the action that the details are blurred.
According to books and movies, the bad man never does the
hero any great harm, so I must have been no hero at all—El

Gezar certainly punished me. He was hard as nails, except for his wind, and there lay my one chance.

The punishment was fifty-fifty, of course; Hank Smith is no kindergarten pupil. None the less, he had me groggy for about ten seconds and started in to gouge my eyes, but I hammered him on the windpipe and got clear. Both of us thought of the dagger, lying there on the floor, at the same instant; he dove for it, but I kicked it out of reach. I caught up the cognac bottle from the table and smashed it squarely over his head, but the thin French glass only cut him up, and he brought up his knee to the groin, then put over his right to my jaw and I went flop into the corner of the room.

When I came down, my outstretched hand fell upon the hilt of the silver dagger.

El Gezar was on top of me like a shot, and landed a kick that doubled me up. Then he dropped to both knees on me and reached for my throat. Through the crimsoned mask of his face his pale eyes were red and terrible.

"I'll tear the damned life out of you!" he panted hoarsely, frothy blood dripping into my eyes from his split lips, and his mustache ragged, blood-soaked. His fingers drove in under my chin, clamped in a grip of iron.

Then, suddenly, he lifted his head and screamed—uttered a great roar that filled the room with billowing waves of sound. My hand had moved, almost spasmodically, even without any conscious brain-control. He loosed me and stood up, the silver haft of the curved Moorish knife protruding from his left side; then his knees bent and he fell over on the floor face down. A long shiver went through his body, as with a fish clubbed on the head, and he lay quiet.

I lay quiet too, for a long while, listening for the sound of voices outside, or for poundings at the door to indicate that his shouts had gained attention by those in the courtyard. Nothing happened. The confusion caused by the bringing in of Si Kalil had evidently drowned out the nature of his bellowings, although his voice must have been heard and known. He had probably given orders not to be disturbed—and no one was anxious to bother him.

Well, he was dead; no doubt whatever about that.

I thought I was done for also; only that dagger coming under my hand had saved me. As it was, I found myself a long way from doing any nimble capering. After getting back some breath and strength, I dragged myself over to the table, where stood a glass half filled with cognac. This burned new life into me, and I sat up—I was unable to stand on my feet for the present, since he had given me a severe mauling.

Aside from the battering, I had no permanent injury, although any immediate exertion was out of the question. I sat there half-conscious, careless of passing time, until I realized that the sharp daylight outside was passing. Then I roused myself and came painfully to my feet, reached for a cigaret, and considered.

It was almost impossible to adhere to my program, as the first attempt at movement showed me; even to walk across the room was a supreme achievement—and any man who meant to take over the management of Helal and its hillmen had to be vigorous, alert, able to handle any man who did not jump at his command. I was done for, until morning at least. Even my brain was dazed by the hammering El Gezar had given me.

I ate some fruit and cakes, emptied a flask of native wine that was on the table, and unbarred the door. Passing down the corridor to the court with the pool, I sat beside the water and bathed my head and hands, getting off the blood and greatly refreshing myself. One eye was closed and probably black, and I knew I must be well marked up otherwise, not to mention my torn clothes. There was no disguising that I had been in a scrap.

However, evening was approaching, and the thought spurred frantically at me, driving me up and along toward the courtyard of the castle. Progress was difficult, but I assumed as careless an air as possible, and reached the courtyard to find it uncomfortably thronged. Si Kalil had been laid on a mat close to that of the blind El Meknezi, and as I drew near I saw that his face was swathed in bandages, as was one leg. He had been pretty badly smashed up, it seemed, and had probably been asleep, for now two men were helping him sit up, while another held a bowl of food; his mouth was free of bandages, so that he could eat and talk.

My appearance caused an immediate stir of interest, and a buzz of talk and laughter. I made my way to the side of Si Kalil. The sun was down by this time, and the call of the muezzin was going up from the mosque below, but none of the garrison departed; they made their prayers here and now, the blind saint with the rest, while I stood waiting. Si Kalil alone did not move, though his voice joined those of the others, and the head of Tellier above the gate grinned down in ghastly fashion at the scene, the ancient singsong prayers to Allah resounding from the massive walls around and re-echoing faintly from the precincts of the mosque.

Presently it was over, the robed figures rising around me, the blind saint back on his mat clutching his rosary, the sky darkening overhead. The momentary pause in life was past, and I leaned over to catch the words of Si Kalil, who could see nothing by reason of his bandages.

"What is it they say, *m'sieu!*" he croaked, fingering a blood-clot in his beard. "That you too are hurt? Where is El Gezar?"

"Drunk," I returned. "He had me send away the woman he had brought here, and then the drink brought madness upon him. He sought to rush out and kill, shouting for blood—this was about the time they brought you back here. So we fought, and he had the worst of it; and now he is asleep. He will be sane enough when he wakens. Where is Hajj Muhammad?"

HE BROKE into excited speech, and the garrison came thronging around, with many a wondering ejaculation. I had to repeat my question several times before he passed it on, and then several men made reply, which he translated.

"Allah alone knows! The holy man and his followers went to

the village early this morning and then departed; they have not been seen since, and none knows where they are. Did El Gezar give no orders?"

I hesitated, lighting a cigaret to gain a moment's time.

Our conversation had drawn the attention of everyone; in the bearded faces around, in the tense silence, was anxiety and suspense which gave me pause. I weighed the chances, and then decided to stake everything on one throw of the dice.

If Si Kalil knew nothing of Maillot's connection with the plot, I had the whole game in my own hands. I could then order out half the garrison to seize Maillot and anyone who came with him. It was a good gamble, with the odds in my favor—the absence of Hajj Muhammad threatened to ruin everything, but I might yet retrieve matters. So, in an evil moment, I took the chance and spoke.

"Yes," I rejoined, feeling him out to see how much he might know. "He said that Maillot and others were on the way here—he meant to have them seized and shot like the spy whose head hangs there above the gate—"

Si Kalil caught his breath sharply.

"Allah! Then he was indeed drunk. You know how this matter concerns Captain Maillot?"

I had lost.

"Naturally," I said, "since he sent me here—"

"And I am stricken at this moment!" A groan broke from Si Kalil, then he uttered sharp commands in Arabic.

I turned aside, edged my way slowly out of the throng, hoping against hope that I might yet do something but it was too late. The throng surged, leaped into action. A dozen men dashed from the courtyard at a run. Two others ranged alongside me, voices rose high, and when I would have started for the gateway, my two guards grinned and motioned me into the castle. A wild yell went up from somewhere inside. They had discovered the body of El Gezar. I had not locked the door of the treasure room.

Ten minutes later I was sitting in a guarded room, while pandemonium swept the *kasbah*.

Well, I had bungled it; and all I could do was to curse the saintly Hajj Muhammad for having let me down. I was in a little bare room with a filthy mat for bed, and obviously a prisoner; presently they brought me in a bowl of *couscousu* for my supper, then departed and left me to darkness. My door was locked, and a high window gave no hope of escape, even had I been in any condition to attempt freedom. I stretched out stiffly on the mat and after a bit fell asleep despite my aches.

When I wakened, it was to find my worst anticipations realized. It was getting on toward morning, as the intense cold informed me. My door was open, and an Arab was holding up a lantern; behind him, looking down at me, stood Maillot—now in native costume, which well became his handsome bronzed features, his jet-black eyes and thin lips. The look which he bent upon me brought me sitting upright—then he waved his hand and was gone, without a word, and the door clanged shut.

What I said, would not go through the mails. If that fool saint had only stuck around, all would now be well, but when he dropped out of sight, my whole scheme had simply piled up to topple over and crush me. However, there was nothing to be done about it. The worst had happened, I had lost the wager, and now the stake had to be paid. So I stretched out again, and wakened no more until the morning sunlight was striking through my high window, and two men were shaking me.

That was a bitter awakening, but after I was on my feet I could walk well enough, and they led me out to the great court yard. Here in the brilliant morning sunlight, burst upon me a splendid scene—which unfortunately, I was not in condition to appreciate.

THE RULER of the place sat beneath a canopy beside the gateway, as was of old the Moroccan custom; this ruler was Maillot, in snow-white robes, and two lordly Arabs sat with him—bearded, stately men, undoubtedly the Said el Wazani and

Si Alem whom I had named in my note to him, the two chiefs in the sultan's circle who were with him in his little schemes. Around were half a dozen of the garrison as guards, while the remainder were formed up in the courtyard, now all in uniform, rifles at side. At the gateway, and outside it, were crowded the folk from the village. And over the gateway hung two fresh heads, while in the open space before the canopy lay two bloody heaps of rags—who they were, what they had done, I never learned. At one side of the three chiefs sat the blind El Meknezi, fingering his rosary. I looked for Hassan, but saw him not.

I was led out facing the three chiefs, and Maillot smiled thinly as he met my eyes. Then two men carried out Si Kalil and set him down, and he spoke out from his bandaged face, in Arabic. When he had finished, others spoke. All that passed, of course, was quite unintelligible to me; I stood waiting, while Maillot asked a few questions, and then conferred with his two friends. They plucked their beards and looked wise, and when they had reached a decision, Maillot announced it in a few curt words. I saw a look of cruel delight flash over the faces of the Arabs, and they broke into a quick yell—a sharp and terrible yelp whose ferocity sent a shiver through my spine. Then Maillot stood up, and silence fell.

"My dear M. Smith!" To my astonishment, Maillot addressed me in English—I had not known that he spoke it. "You are adjudged guilty of killing El Gezar and of attempting to betray this place and its secrets. Have you anything to say?"

"Only that I wish I'd done for you when I had the chance," I returned. There was no use in beating about the bush or asking for mercy.

"Then you are condemned to die by the punishment of salt," he said, and sat down. "Not," he added, "until you have had a little conversation with us in private. There are one or two questions we desire to ask you, my friend."

He gave an order, and the ranks broke up, with joyful yells. My guards jerked me away, and as I went, I saw the holy El Meknezi stand up and address Maillot. A lot of good his holiness had done me! It would be more to the point that Solomon sent some emissary with two good eyes and a knowledge of French.

I was conducted into El Gezar's favorite spot, evidently chosen for the interview—an alcove opening upon the courtyard with its orange trees and pool and splashing fountains. I sank down wearily upon the rugs and waited. I knew perfectly well what this punishment of salt meant, and all I wanted was to get hold of a weapon and go out like a man. To have my palms slit up and across, covered with salt, then bound in green bullock-hide and sewed tight—to suffer until the rotting flesh drove me into stark insanity—no, that was no way for Hank Smith to die!

Maillot and his two friends came sauntering along, and made themselves comfortable on the cushions at one side of the alcove. After them came El Meknezi, led by one of the garrison and conducted respectfully to a seat by the entrance arch. By his side squatted down another Arab with reed pen, inkpot and paper, and began to write busily while the holy man mumbled, evidently in dictation. His voice was scarcely heard, so low was it.

Now Maillot spoke to me in French. He had not wanted Si Kalil to overhear what we said, of course, and nobody else knew French here except the two chiefs with him.

"Now, *mon ami!* Let us clear up a few things, while they prepare the bullock hide and the salt," and he smiled at me in his direct, cruel fashion. "These two guards have orders to shoot you at any move to escape, so when we have talked a little, you can very easily obtain a more speedy death than that to which you are doomed. Do you comprehend?"

"Perfectly," I responded. "Perhaps you have a cigaret to spare?"

"But yes," and producing a case, he gave one of the two guards a cigaret for me. I had matches, and lighted it. The two grave chieftains watched me curiously. "I can now understand that you have played a very slippery game, M. Smith," resumed Maillot, "and you played it very well. Was it at the command of your fat little Englishman, M. Solomon?"

"More or less, yes," I returned. "It looks as though I had lost, however."

"I agree with you," and he laughed. "Your ruse nearly succeeded; from what I can gather, you got us here in order to let Hajj Muhammad know where we stood—eh? Well, rest assured, I have sent messengers to that blessed *santon*, assuring him that I am taking the place of El Gezar, and asking him to come here and deal frankly with me. I must of course change my plans somewhat, thanks to your interference. I should like to have seen your fight with El Gezar! Perhaps you can tell us what has become of Hassan, the son of El Biskri?"

"Why do you want him?" I demanded. "To kill him?"

Maillot laughed. "Of course not, simpleton. He is to become the next sultan."

"Oh! Well, you should know where he is. It was Hassan who brought you my note."

"What?" Maillot and the two chieftains were startled by this. "You mean it?"

"Certainly," I returned. "And Hassan does not care to join your little plot or let himself be used by you—"

There was a sudden wild yell, and we all looked around. The scribe who had been squatting beside El Meknezi had leaped to his feet, eyes staring, fright and horror in his face. He was waving the paper on which he had been writing; and suddenly, whirling around, he went dashing off and was gone.

"What the devil!" exclaimed Maillot, and uttered a laugh.

Then I saw something curious. The blind saint had taken out a little clay pipe and was stuffing tobacco into it. Somehow, his action reminded me of something I could not quite place. He scratched a match and held it to his pipe—and then his eyes opened, eyes of a placid and expressionless sky-blue, and fastened upon Maillot. I uttered one gasp of astounded recognition.

"No, sir, it ain't the devil," he said in English. "It's me, instead—and werry 'appy I am to meet you, sir."

Maillot gaped at him blankly.

"What? You—who are you? You speak English?"

"Yes, sir," and Solomon rose, with his wheezy chuckle. "I'm that 'ere fat little Englishman as you was just now a-speaking of, sir, and I'd like to 'ave a bit o' speech with you, sir, just like that."

It was true—incredibly true. This saint was John Solomon himself!

CHAPTER XIX

MAILLOT'S END

MAILLOT WAS dumbfounded. The two chieftains with him shot out swift questions in French, but he paid no heed. Staring at Solomon, he reverted to his own tongue.

"You—you are M. Solomon? But this is incredible, impossible!"

"Not at all," said Solomon, with another chuckle. He spoke French as fluently as Arabic, and much more correctly than English. Then he turned to me, a twinkle in his blue eyes. "I 'opes, sir, as that 'ere Hajj Muhammad ain't discommoded you, so to speak. If I ain't mistook, we'll 'ear 'im any moment now—"

Maillot, recovering from his astounded daze, shot out a sharp command. One of the two guards hesitated, then strode to Solomon and swiftly frisked him unavailingly. No weapon was produced. Solomon puffed calmly at his pipe, and showed a little red notebook which he held in one hand.

"I'd be werry glad if you'd see fit to look over this 'ere statement of me accounts, sir," he said, holding out the notebook. "I expect as 'ow you'll find everything entered up, all shipshape and Bristol fashion. That 'ere scribe, 'e went and lost 'is 'ead when it come to putting of it in Arabic—"

The guard took the notebook and gave it to Maillot, who stared for a moment at Solomon and then glanced down, opening the little red book and frowning at it. I recalled the terrified scream of the scribe and his abrupt flight, and now I heard a chorus of voices welling up from the castle courtyard—shrill, high voices of men amazed and terrified. What did it all mean?

Maillot turned over the pages of the little book, scornfully.

"Blagues!" he exclaimed. "All nonsense—"

His voice died. Suddenly he changed countenance; his eyes were distended, a frightful and inexplicable pallor swept into his face. What was it that he saw there on the notebook page? I never knew. With an oath of furious rage, he threw up his arm and flung the little red notebook through the air, hurled it out so that it fell into the pool in the court.

"A lie!" he cried out, and shook his fist at Solomon. "You lie!"

"No, sir," said Solomon calmly, although the two Arab chiefs had come to their feet with hot questions. "No, sir. Providence is a werry mysterious thing, Cap'n Maillot; if so be as it 'its you, then you're done for, and if it don't 'it you, then nothing can 'urt you—"

One of the garrison officers came running, panting, his eyes rolling. He shouted something in Arabic—something that held Maillot paralyzed, that sent the two chieftains into evident consternation and alarm.

"Yes, sir," said Solomon. "If I was you, I'd go and see about it—Hajj Muhammad and five 'undred men a-pouring into this 'ere castle ain't to be sneezed at—"

From somewhere came a shot, then a ragged volley, then the shouts of men and a continuous burst of firing. Maillot ripped out an oath and then sprang past me, dragging a pistol from beneath his *jellab;* the two Arabs screamed after him, then followed hastily. The guards lifted their pistols irresolutely; Solomon took the pipe from his mouth and gave them a sharp command in Arabic, they too departed at a run.

We were alone there in the alcove, while the *kasbah* resounded to a bursting drumfire of shots and a pandemonium of voices.

"Good lord!" I exclaimed, staring at the placid-eyed figure of Solomon. "What's happened?"

"Well, sir, a lot 'as 'appened since yesterday, as the old gent said

when 'e kissed the pretty 'ousemaid," and he chuckled wheezily. "It was me as sent that 'ere Hajj Muhammad off to bring in
'is men, just like that, and mop up this here crowd. You see, sir,
the Resident 'as appointed a 'igh court, so to speak, with 'im at
the 'ead of it, to look into all the cases of injustice and so on.
Then Hassan come back ahead o' Maillot, and that showed Hajj
Muhammad we 'ad told 'im the truth—"

"What?" I cried. "You mean to say he brought in his men and
is wiping out this crowd?"

"Just like that, sir," said Solomon placidly. "And if I was you,
I'd set werry tight, sir. You and me are in a werry ticklish place—"

A gasping, strangled yell drowned out his words. A man
appeared in the archway, fell forward on his face, and slid headlong into the wall, where he lay quiet. From his hand a pistol
skittered across the tiles, and I plunged for it. After him, a whole
irruption of uniformed figures flooded across the open court—
hillmen of the garrison, firing rapidly, falling among the orange
trees and into the pool, wiped out by a spray of lead from automatic rifles. In pursuit of them came and went a second flood
of figures—Arabs, this time in white jellabs, Hajj Muhammad's
men. I stood with the pistol in my hand, watching them disap-
pear across the court, all save the dead and dying. What hell was
going on in the castle courtyard below could only be guessed.

And then, suddenly, Maillot appeared—running, stripped
of his robes, a gash of crimson across his forehead, his face
converted in a snarl of furious desperation. He saw us there
and whirled about, his pistol lifting.

"Name of a dog!" he panted hoarsely. "You, at least—" There
was a sharp report, then another—but not from his pistol. I was
hardly conscious that I had fired. Maillot spun about, then his
knees loosened and he fell heavily.

"Dang it!" exclaimed Solomon. "Now look what you've went
and done—dang it! And we was particular set on taking 'im
back alive—"

I laughed, a little wildly. Without warning, a strange half-naked figure, unarmed, long hair flying, confronted us—I recognized Hajj Muhammad, his frenzied features frightful to see as he barked out something at Solomon, waved his arms, and went running on.

"Well, sir," said Solomon calmly, "that ends it—been and took the castle, 'e 'as! Them there men of 'is 'ad their rifles a-going before the garrison could get armed, and werry lucky as they did, says I. Now let's you and me, Mr. Smith, take that 'ere gold and give it to Miss Pontois, and then we'll 'ave a bit of rest in Marrakesh. And on account o' what you've been and done, sir, I wouldn't be surprised if the Resident was to up and give you the Legion of Honor or one o' them 'ere medals—"

He did, too—but all that came after the end of the stray.

ABOUT THE AUTHOR

H. BEDFORD-JONES is a Canadian by birth, but not by profession, having removed to the United States at the age of one year. For over twenty years he has been more or less profitably engaged in writing and traveling. As he has seldom resided in one place longer than a year or so and is a person of retiring habits, he is somewhat a man of mystery; more than once he has suffered from unscrupulous gentlemen who impersonated him—one of whom murdered a wife and was subsequently shot by the police, luckily after losing his alias.

The real Bedford-Jones is an elderly man, whose gray hair and precise attire give him rather the appearance of a retired foreign diplomat. His hobby is stamp collecting, and his collection of Japan is said to be one of the finest in existence. At present writing he is en route to Morocco, and when this appears in print he will probably be somewhere on the Mojave Desert in company with Erle Stanley Gardner.

Questioned as to the main facts in his life, he declared there was only one main fact, but it was not for publication; that his life had been uneventful except for numerous financial losses, and that his only adventures lay in evading adventurers. In his younger years he was something of an athlete, but the encroachments of age preclude any active pursuits except that of motoring. He is usually to be found poring over his stamps, working at his typewriter, or laboring in his California rose garden, which is one of the sights of Cathedral Cañon, near Palm Springs.

www.ingramcontent.com/pod-product-compliance
Lightning Source LLC
Chambersburg PA
CBHW050128030726
47505CB00007B/2080